BLAMING THE VICTIM

JACKSON RATEAU

ISBN: 978-1-63821-623-0 (Paperback Edition)
ISBN: 978-1-63821-624-7 (Hardcover Edition)
ISBN: 978-1-63821-622-3 (E-book Edition)

Some characters and events in this book are fictitious. Any similarity to the real persons, living or dead, is coincidental and not intended by the author.

Book Ordering Information

Phone Number: 315 288-7939 ext. 1000 or 347-901-4920
Email: info@globalsummithouse.com
Global Summit House
www.globalsummithouse.com

Printed in the United State of America

Fabrication and propagation of the HIV virus throughout the world is an atrocious crime against humanity. Why have the victims of the disease become the accused?

This book is dedicated to my father Grandoit Rateau, my sons Dave J Rateau and Max Daniel Rateau, my daughters Neev N Rateau and Christina D Rateau, my brother Jean Ulrick Rateau, my sister Fisline Rateau and my friend Dunès Ducrépin.

Thanks to Mr. William Pierre. Spurred on by team and partnership spirit, he freely helped me to realize the translation of this book.

To avoid being led like beasts to the slaughterhouse, we have to learn about this world and its leaders.

"I found myself between two centuries as at the confluence of two rivers; I plunged into their troubled waters, regretfully leaving the ancient shores where I was born and swimming hopefully toward the unknown shore where new generation will land".

François René de Chateaubriand

Good stories have been narrated, written, or engraved on rocks for eternity. Like their authors, they remain immortal.

The author wrote a transparent story from a fertile imagination in which characters evolved with realism. Literature that is rich in characters, drama, and realities cannot die.

This novel is indeed a story of life and death, a mélange in which reality is a component. The novel also transforms reality into fiction to explain what the author feels and observes.

Blaming the Victim is the result of intriguing research, which brings to light pertinent information to counter a malicious, abominable and baseless accusation. Denouncing the crimes of scoundrels becomes routine for innocent.

HIV, the disease hatched in the laboratories of Fort Detrick, Maryland has already decimated millions of men, women and children all over the planet, while millions of others afflicted by this disease await death.

Whatever the reason, the powerful cannot always be right, because the virus is still alive.

CHAPTER I

It was the second day of spring, which had returned yesterday on the twenty-first of March. The temperature was neither warm nor cold, but mild. The trees showed their first buds. The entire city was bathed in midday sunshine like a colorful daffodil. As usual, the streets were not yet crowded. They stretched like long gray ribbons, brightened here and there by traffic lights.

The man who drove the pearl gray car was nervous. He stepped on the gas as the light turned yellow. A car began to enter the intersection from his right. He slammed on the brakes, skidding to a stop as the light turned red. He tried to compose himself.

- Something is wrong with me today. I'm not thinking clearly. He pulled out a CD from his favorite Haitian band, Nu Look, and pushed it into the player. A soft melody pulsed out of the speakers, simultaneously relaxing and stimulating him. A trembling sax line expressed misery. The singer explained:

My life is a mystery
an endless illusion
Love in the past
Is my one consolation
If fate would let me choose
I would never cry
Neither pain nor sorrow
would obstruct my happiness
I don't believe in fatalism
I rather believe in fight
I don't believe in pessimism
I rather believe in optimism
I don't believe in giving up
I rather believe in going on
I am ready to love
even though it's in vain

It was the classic love lament of a Kreyòl poem, pure lyrics touching the hearts of sorrow-filled, pained and abandoned souls.

Oh God, why me?
Why am I always miserable?
Always complaining
Even though I am not wrong?
O no no no no
I'm not demanding too much

I would only hope she understands me
That she would love me
I would give her a very warm welcome....

Love is a double-edged sword
a necessary evil
Without love, life is a hell
a pact with Lucifer
To try is not a sin
I won't give up
I'll be happy one day
There is no pain without help
God will take care of me

This was one of his favorite songs from Nu-Look. He sat listening to it, his eyes closed, even after he had finished parking in front of his house. Then he got out of the car, checked his mailbox. He found mostly junk mail, which he never took the time to read. He'd learned the tricks carried in the U.S. mail: official-looking envelopes that contained advertisements, or authoritative-looking letters from fly-by-night companies. And, of course, the bills: phone, electricity, rent, etc. Most of the envelopes ended up in the garbage.

As he prepared to gather tonight's mail, the distinctive name of his insurance company on an envelope caught his eye. He grabbed it and placed it on the dining room table. He pulled a pack of cigarettes from his jean jacket. He took out a cigarette, raised it to the left corner of his lips and lit it. He was going to open the envelope. From his mouth, he removed the cigarette and powerfully exhaled the smoke. The cloud rose up and faded away. He opened the envelope and then pulled out the crinkling paper.

- What! He cried out, with his eyes opening wide. No! I can't believe it.

He read the check again and carefully examined the name on it: Dorven Marc Forest.

- Maybe it's a mistake.

He put the check back in the envelope and put it on the table. The cigarette was already finished. He lit another and pulled a long drag.

- Let me examine it carefully, he thought, maybe I am wrong.

He put on his glasses, pulled out the check, and read it carefully, letter by letter, number by number: "Pay to the order of Dorven Marc Forest the amount of one million one hundred thousand and ninety nine dollars."

He grabbed the phone to call someone; then he changed his mind.

- It's a surprise that could break my heart if it turns out to be a mistake, he thought, a real shock.

For four years, he'd been waiting for an insurance payment of a mere thirty-four hundred dollars. He'd long since given up and had all, but forgotten about it.

- One million one hundred thousand dollars! He exclaimed to himself. Let me call my lawyer, immediately.

With trembling hands, he dialed the number.

- Hello.

- Hello, yes! Good evening. May I speak to Attorney Merlyn please? It's very important.

- Hold on please, said the secretary with a nice voice.

- Hello, this is Merlyn. I'm here to serve you, he heard his lawyer say.

- I'm happy to find you this late, my dear Merlyn. This is Dorven. I hope you recognized my voice.

- Absolutely Mr. Dorven. I was just going to call you….

- Oh yes, about what?

- It's about…okay, you speak first.

- It seemed a little strange, so I thought I'd let you know, Mr. Merlyn. My insurance company issued a check to the order of Mr. Dorven Marc Forest. I found it in my mailbox this afternoon.

- Yes, I am aware of that. This was done at my request and due to my pressure, and the case was easily won. Congratulations…and my thanks also, Mr. Dorven.

- You're welcome, Attorney Merlyn, and I thank you too.

He remained quiet for a moment.

- You know what, Mr. Merlyn?

- No! What?

- I'm afraid.

- Afraid of what?

- I don't know, but I am afraid.

- I understand. It is emotional. Just calm down and everything will be fine, rest assured.

- Excuse me, Mr. Merlyn. I have someone else calling me on the other line.

- Just a second, Mr. Dorven. How much is the amount of your check?

- It's one million, one hundred thousand and ninety-nine dollars.

Dorven was distracted by the other line.

- Hello! Hello!

- Hello Dorven, this is Jude.

- Oh! Jude, Jude! I…I'll call you back.

His brain was muddled. He thought about a thousand things at once. He forgot where he put his bag. He went crazy looking for it everywhere; he had left it in the car. He ran in the bedroom and returned quickly to the living room, where he stood for a moment and then sat on the sofa; he stretched his legs and laid his head on a small cushion. He was thinking about what to do and how to use that money.

- Oh, I see, I'll try to hire an accountant.

Then he thought that wasn't the right idea, He changed his mind. Why hire someone to get involved in his private affairs and pay him so much money? This is something he must think about—think twice about.

Perhaps a few hours of rest would be good for him, if he could sleep. He went to bed. His head was so confused that even the strongest sleeping pill would not put him to sleep. He imagined a trip by car, but may be an accident he couldn't avoid would be fatal. Finally, he later decided to go to a club in Manhattan. Once there, he sat at his table with a bottle of Scotch, his only companion. The hum of the bass throbbed. Girls were crazy, swaying their bodies under the alternating lights of blue and scarlet. Clothing was a feature of the dance hall: leather and wool pants, tight short skirts, bodices shimmering iridescent with sequins, a lot of narrow jeans and long boots.

A bar girl passed near the table like a cat coming to rub against her owner's foot. She grabbed his arm and eventually took him to a bedroom. He spent the night, cuddling the girl in the soft bed.

A few hours before leaving the club, he thought of a new car. On his way back, he stopped at the BMW dealer to negotiate buying an X5 BMW. When he returned home, his mailbox once again was full of mail. This time, he deviated from his bad habit of throwing the mail away without reading it. In fact, he became curious about these letters, and was about to read them. But the days are never the same. Life is the scene of all tragedies. Joy is often fleeting and happiness is the flash of a second. Vanity of vanities, all is vanity, says the wise man. Misfortune always follows a happy day; this is why we can live our lives in perpetual anxiety.

CHAPTER II

The mail from his doctor informs him that the HIV test reveals disease. According to the results—positive—it's clear that the virus has caused extensive damage. His immune system is seriously depleted. Very important, he must meet the doctor about eight.

- What! What is this nonsense? I can't believe it. It would be better to drop it in the garbage can, this fucking mail.

The news is a violent shock, affecting his entire life. Such is life—bizarre, he thought.

- Yesterday I was very happy, too happy. I was confused, not knowing what to do. Yesterday I received the insurance check and I was happy because of my wealth. But today I became the most unfortunate person in the world. I have to see my doctor first.

His life felt short-circuited. At first, he rejects the positive HIV test. But deep down, he accepts his status. In the meantime, he exists between laughter and tears, joy and sadness, life and death, love and hate, wealth and poverty.

His appointment with the doctor was scheduled for the first Wednesday in April. Already it seemed that the atmosphere of death had engulfed him. It was disastrous, catastrophic, and lamentable.

The clinic had been recently painted white. A white fence surrounded the building. The clinic was above the basement to pretend that it was on the second floor. A green lawn had a few scattered trees trembling with the breeze.

Dorven gathered all his strength and tried hard to appear in good health. Everything seems strange to him. He believes in life, in this beautiful and charming world that he will soon leave. The plants seem to be more wondrous than ever to him. In the clinic, it seemed as if everyone already knew him. Everything seemed upside down. It's true this is a clinic, but all the patients in the waiting room did not look sick. They were healthy, even fat. He saw beautiful young people, beautiful girls. They are happy, these people, he thinks. They do not feel condemned with this terrible weight of death.

Now is Dorven's turn. The smiling secretary led him to the doctor. At first he was disappointed, even repelled by the purple paint in the exam room. It was a color he never liked. He became frustrated and touchy. He figured that he was put in this room because of his disease. He also noticed a change in the doctor's mood from last time. He was smiling and seemed nicer. I can understand that—seeing me so bad, nearly dead, he has mercy on me. The doctor, sharp in his white shirt, stethoscope around his neck, really was looking at him with pity and compassion.

- How are you my friend? The doctor greeted him with a serene smile, tinged with concern.

- I don't feel well, Doctor. My head is killing me.

- I see Mr. Dorven, I see. I am sorry about your health, but as a doctor I have to tell the truth.

- I think that's right; I am not mad at you. But I would like you to be more explicit about the development of this virus.

- For example?

- My damaged organs, the condition of my immune system—in short, my life expectancy.

- Well, honestly the worst part of your situation is that your blood type leaves you vulnerable. You are less and less resistant to the virus. The damage is enormous, sir. I am sorry to say, but I am convinced that with drugs and discipline, you can live up to two years.

He looks at the doctor, perplexed and despairing.

- And with sex?

- Sex—you might be good for fifteen months, but with a calm mind.

- Calm mind, what do you mean?

- Relaxation, positive thoughts, recreation will help you cope with the situation. No alcohol and tobacco.

After their short dialogue, the doctor gave him a bag of various medicines.

He left the clinic, almost running. He opened the car door with the remote control, sat behind the wheel. Thinking about what the doctor said put him in the depths of a bottomless pit, without a glimmer of hope. He couldn't control his thoughts. His sex life had been always troubled. The only person he remembered having sex with was a white girl, Marrey Skotth.

- Marrey Skotth, shit, he says nervously, that fucking bitch, only her. She gave me this disease. Fuck you Marrey Skotth! Fuck you again!

Wanting to control his remaining days in his own way, of course, he was determined:

- I am the violent wind that can raise every particle of dust. Wherever I go I will take a lot of girls—a lot of people with me. My money will be spent until the last cent. I am a calm madman who will fool all women, [*yon bakoulou malad*].

CHAPTER III

The man who is good-looking and badly behaved is a terrible hawk with talons of death.

The last time he was in the city he wore a dark grey suit and was carrying a paper bag. He is a very handsome and sexual person. His torso is svelte. His hair is jet black, cut in the back like a knife blade. His thick eyebrows sprang up and his eyes were shining like crystal. He always appeared calm, but a little cool. This attitude reflected his charisma, or the force that connected his soul to others. Even a dog he met by chance ignored his owner to run after him. He was such a specimen of his race. Any woman would go after him, take him to decorate her house.

He had neither wife nor children. He practiced yoga and was a masochist about physical fitness. He had a hidden life. He was peaceful and nice, but never smiled. He did not have many friends. He enjoyed a nocturnal life. For some time he had not been working on a daily basis. His life was debauchery and relaxation. His original name was Venord. He didn't like the name given by his mother. He called himself Dorven, his new name, before he became a U.S. citizen.

The man was walking along the street. He passed a woman before the cross walk and went into the sex store. He bought pictures of naked women and pornographic books and the like. On the way back home he was serene. He took some old photographs down to make room for new ones on the wall. The interior was spacious. A blue light kept the room lit always. The floor was carpeted in green with black rows of birds and drawings of women. The room smelled fresh and inviting.

The day was gone. A lovely young woman was driving fast, hair in the wind. She was crazy, going to her first date. First date? Yes first, because since returning from Haiti the day after her marriage three months ago, she had no desire to taste her husband's love or offer him her sweetness. The unhappy husband swallowed all this against his will. She had a big dilemma; she had betrayed her heart. She was pretty like a flower the day she met the poisonous hawk. She was appreciated by a few smiling guys; for her, it was casual. She had decided not to pay attention to them. Dorven was the chosen one who could open her heart. She was happy to surrender. They were talking, chatting on the phone, and she finally agreed. She was hurrying because she didn't want miss out on that love affair. She definitely needed it.

The man was going to concentrate on his yoga when the phone rang three times. Slowly he picked it up, waited a few moments.

- Hello.

- Yes, hello! She says with her heart wide open, this is Mary Lyn, and I'm coming over.

- Oh, well, very well. Where are you now?

- Right at your house, by the entrance.

- Wait a little while sweetie; I'm coming right away.

Quickly he rearranged things. He gathered the scattered pills, hid them in a drawer. He checked again to make sure there was no suspicious stuff in the room. He walked to the door and pressed the buzzer. Outside Mary Lyn was impatient.

Her first time in a bachelor flat, she was impressed, but uncomfortable with the pornographic display.

- Is someone else living here with you?

- No, he answered amazed, eyes wide, why?

- Nothing.

She was shy, too shy.

- You know, I…I apologize.

- Why?

- You know, see, I forget your name.

- Dorven.

- True, Dorven, she repeated timidly.

- See, you are not comfortable. I can't understand why you have forgotten my name.

- You're right; I'm not completely at ease. I hope you understand. Forgive me, I'm sorry.

She was quiet a few minutes, and started again.

- Why did you insist that I come over here?

- Why?

- Yes, why?

- Because we had no choice. Your house is too crowded, too hard to get to. Remember you told me that?

- Yes, and that's the truth.

- Well, I'm right?

Feeling conflicted; she stood up, consulting her watch.

- Three months ago, I was in Haiti for my wedding, she began to say. She was silent for a moment to stare at a man's picture on the wall.

- For some reason, I didn't go through with it, she confessed. I came back a virgin.

- So, what happened then?

- Well, my heart disapproved of my decision. I had to marry the guy so he could enter the U.S.

- So, you have to go back to Haiti?

- Yes, soon.

- Do you like my flat?

- Beautiful, beautiful, especially the bedroom. But I don't…oh, I am sorry.

- Don't be sorry. Will you accept my kiss Mary Lyn?

- What, your kiss?

- Yes, so what?

- I don't know.

He bent down to her, touched her hair, and kissed her lips….They lay down on the bed, kissed for a few minutes. Suddenly, Dorven got up, opened a drawer and took out a liquid for him and the girl….She thought her flesh had been cut because of the heavy bleeding. It was her broken hymen instead.

The moon was brightening the sky when she decided to leave. And the man handed her an envelope containing a check for five thousand dollars.

- What is this for? She asked curiously, her face disturbed.

- Nothing…just a little present.

- Present? I don't understand. Do you think I came here to sell myself to you? Am I a prostitute?

- I…I just wanted to pay for your virginity.

- Five thousand dollars is the price of my love? Even five million dollars could not buy it. Don't you dare, you rat!

- What is the price then?

- The price is true love, conscience, nothing else. Looking at the check with disdain she added, and commitment to share a common life. A woman's virginity is too precious to be sold. She tore it all, the envelope and check, threw it in a trashcan—she left very angrily. She returned violently.

- I am not a whore, you know.

- I apologize, Miss Mary Lyn; whores are my favorites. We get alone very well.

- You rotten nasty guy!

CHAPTER IV

Dorven Marc Forest had lived in the U.S. for more than two decades. Despite that he was the oldest of the children he didn't have any attachment to his parents. They couldn't count on him. Thus, on the insistence of his mother, his father capitulated. He risked smuggling trip to send the sixteen year-old boy to Miami Beach. After a few unproductive years there, he moved to New York. He had lived in Queens, Brooklyn and Manhattan.

The old man struggled to make a living, to get rid of the debt for his son, who had never been in touch, not even a phone call. His father and mother, his brothers and sister were still living in poverty. They were crowded into a small room, in the heart of an old shantytown infested with mud, flies, cockroaches and all kinds of pests. The miserable slum was like a hell in northern Port-au-Prince since the childhood of Madam Colo. Mr. Germain Marc Forest didn't mind whether his creditors took him to court and eventually to jail. He had to spend whatever he could to save his son. However Dorven didn't care at all about those he left behind more than a quarter of a century ago. *Dèyè do se nan ginen[once one left home, forget about all behind].* He was such a one for escape. He never suffered from loneliness or nostalgia. He is a selfish guy, lives only for himself as if in a vacuum.

Everything was ready for his trip to Haiti; the motherland without winter, with its dazzling brilliant sun, its streets populated with smiling young girls. The agency in charge of Dorven's trip arranged a car and rented him a superb house. It was a quiet house, in the middle of dense greenery, landscaped with flowers, surrounded by bushes and tall trees in an agreeable area of Furcy on the heights of Pétion-Ville, commonly called "at the top." This is bourgeois territory, forbidden to poor people unless they are gardeners or maids. He sent expensive furnishings, and clothes and accessories were also shipped.

He was looking forward to being there, inflated by the abundance of his wealth and extravagance of the world. It's true, he is the son of a slum in Port-au-Prince, but nothing can prevent him from being one of those rich men, savoring the delights of this great world, which he had always heard about without ever enjoying. Now the time has come to show off his wealth. All those years out of the country severed his relations with the small universe of people living hopelessly in abject poverty since the day he left this country in a large *canter*— a dealer's boat.

At sixteen he was the dream, the hope, of all in his family and even those to come. Unfortunately after twenty-fiveyears, he seems to have forgotten everything; ignorant in a country that is no longer familiar. Getting girls, living wild was the gift he intended to give himself. He thought about Marie Lyn for a while; he blamed himself, acting so stupidly by offering money in exchange for affection. When he remembered that she was already infected like him, he felt satisfied. She was really bleeding that day, he remembered.

He had entered the U.S. young, poor, his head filled with ambition. He had been very healthy. Now, twenty-five years later, he will leave the country rich, but sick, infected, without hope for living. He flashed back his youth in Bel-Air. He was only a teenager when he left the country and never returned. That's why he could recall nothing, couldn't even remember his parents and his friends. Nothing is left in his memory.

Finally, everything was in order for his departure: funds transferred to a bank in Haiti, apartment vacated, luggage weighed and ticket confirmed.

The night before he left some friends gave him a dinner party in a nice catering hall in Brooklyn. He was so surprised he didn't even know how to greet and thank his guests. His friends let him know that he wasn't supposed to worry about it because he was a guest too. Only one of his friends was aware of his illness, and he kept it secret.

Everyone had his opinion and criticism about his sudden decision to leave the country in such extravagance. Because not many people knew about his personal life, they started speculating. Some said with absolute certainty that he won the lottery for the exorbitant sum of twelve million. Others argued that he made it from drugs; he joined the cartel. Verbal warfare caused a bloody brawl between the quarrelers. Gerard confirmed without reservation that he knows about Tiguy.

- Yes man, he says in a hard tone, Tiguy is in the cartel, I know. How could he trade his Toyota Camry just four months old for a Hummer?

- He signed a check my dear, what's so abnormal to you?

- No, persisted another, furious, swearing that: *Tonè kraze m [I swear to God]*, it's not true. What kind of job is this guy Tiguy doing to sign a check of sixty-five thousand dollars for a Hummer? You must be crazy to believe such bullshit.

They were inside a barber shop when Mary came in, a tease who claims to be a Cap-Haitian native. She was always talking, even if she didn't know what to say sometimes.

- This man wants to go back to Haiti to spend his money? He'll regret it. He'll be assassinated, I bet you. I'm telling you guys, Haiti is my country, but forgets about it. I'm living in United States, a blessed country. My children are American-born citizens. Me too, I'm an American citizen. I have my house, two cars and a bank account of one thousand dollars at least. What more do I need?

Already, the dispute is too loud and then another started swearing louder.

- You get on my nerves, man. Why should I lie to you? What do you have to bribe me? I can swear on my children's lives that Dorven managed a major coup in the cartel, and he won big money.

- You lie like a dog.

- I'm telling the truth, you are the ignorant one who says nonsense.

-Stop speaking to me like that. Don't say anything to me now.

- Who are you to owe respect to? Fuck you, stupid.

- Fuck you, stupid! Stop talking crap, slamming him hard in the face.

The other hit him back with a big punch on the mouth. Then they kicked and bit and punched each other.

A passer-by who saw the scene began to sound a horn and hum. The instrument was eighty-five centimeters long and came from an animal called codo, native to the desert of Yemen.

Some customers rushed to help, but vainly. Only the intervention of police had put an end to the fight by arresting both men.

CHAPTER V

Rigid tail, wings stretched and beak forward, the metallic bird took off, crossing the air. The sea through the windows seemed a mix of white and gray clouds, as if it were sky. Sparkling purple light spread. In the infinite distance, forests appeared as green spots and the land looked red. The mechanical bird continued its route. The passengers did not feel it moving. Some white tourists were sleeping comfortably in their seats. Others were busy reading magazines or books. The Haitian passengers were tired of the long travel and couldn't wait to get there. Fortunately, the plane didn't take long to descend. La Gonave appeared as a small dark plate on the ocean. The bare peaks of the mountains were pale and immense. Finally the plane came near Port-Au-Prince, which looked like a basin with gray and rusted roofs. It passed over the blackish pond of "Source Puante". A voice, thin but with charm, echoed through the plane.

- Attention ladies and gentlemen, we're about to land in Toussaint Louverture International Airport at Port-Au-Prince. It's actually one o'clock seventeen minutes and forty-three seconds. The temperature is thirty-four degrees Celsius, ninety-three Fahrenheit. What a beautiful sunny day! We had a very excellent trip. We thank you for choosing American Airlines. Stay in your seats until the landing is complete.

Dorven's heart was jumping. He has returned to Haiti after some twenty-five years outside the country. His father and mother, though old, are still alive. He is the eldest of five brothers and one sister. Sabine, the youngest, is twenty-three. Finally he has arrived in the country, unable to recognize a single person. The agency was to have sent two employees to pick him up at the airport. The first passengers began to come out. They lined up with bags in their hands, attaché cases and packs on their backs. They went from counter to counter and had the wait was not very long. Dorven's eyes were everywhere, searching around him in vain. Everything was strange and unfamiliar: the attitude of the employees, how they work and the misery on their faces. Beggars were everywhere inside. At the arrival gate it was a mess, noisy. Some people tried to grab passengers' suitcases. The luggage carousel was antiquated, dilapidated with missing plates. It was terribly hot. The passengers kept their eyes on their luggage. A nice girl walked around the carousel. She wore a pair of black and gold glasses. Her black hair, very smooth, fell down her back and was fastened by a silver barrette. She was pure black. Her clean face reflected a rare beauty. She was an ideal woman, lovely to everyone. Her elegant gait, the light in her eyes, was entrancing.

Dorven, the alert hunter, as well as everyone else, had seen her. She looked at him furtively, and then by chance their eyes met, like opposite electrical charges. She was on the opposite side of the carousel. Suddenly the luggage came around. Dorven started grabbing his. She hurried to stop him; a trolley was close by.

- I'm sorry sir; she said with a certain quiet boldness, it's my job to do the loading.

He resisted vainly for a moment. He never thought that such a charming girl would have a job handling luggage in the airport.

- How much I owe you, my dear?
- It's up to you sir.

The crowd was very dense, sweating. A lady near them was sighing while fanning her chest with both hands.

Dorven pulled out his wallet and handed her two $100 bills.

- Tell me who are you? He asked.
- What, who am I?
- Yes, I'm sorry, I would say…like, what's your name?
- Adélina.
- I am Dorven. I am happy to meet you.
- Likewise.
- Can I have your number?
- My number? She remained quiet, thinking. After a few minutes she agreed.

The man wrote the number in his notebook.

- I don't have yours, she says cynically.

- You're right, I'm sorry. Unfortunately, I just arrived; I don't have a phone number yet. So I'll call you tonight.

They remained quiet a moment, and then he added:

- I need your help.

- My help, she repeats surprised, how?

- I must call my agency, could you help me to find a phone?

- Just one moment.

She opened her handbag, pulled out her cell and handed it to him, adjusting her glasses, which almost fell off.

- Thank you a thousand times goddess, he said, contemplating her exciting sensuous body.

- Hello! Hello! This is Dorven. I came to the airport about an hour ago. I can't find your men. Would you please give me some clues so I can identify them? And the voice on the phone:

- There are two men at the airport to pick you up Mr. Dorven. They wear blue jeans, black t-shirts with badges with the name of the agency. It's easy sir.

- Do they have a phone with them?

- Of course sir, can you take the number now?

The girl had already a piece of paper and a pen.... he found them.

- Well! I must leave immediately Adélina.

Outside, the waves of heat wave made the air dance. Wind from the east ruffled the leaves and the sun was shinning under an immense blue sky. They could barely make it through the packed crowd.

CHAPTER VI

Port-au-Prince at one in the afternoon is in a class by itself. The temperature is nearly one hundred degrees. Some vehicles are going slowly. The diffused rays of the sun bounce off glass like yellow flames. The street vendors are all over, crying out their goods. Some people are begging for food. Students are on their way back to school. Factory workers hurry back to work after a light meal. It is a moving city. The street proceeds straight to the black metal fence circling the front of the building. Above a sign on a black board indicates Toussaint Louverture International Airport.

The jeep smoothly moved south, then went around the traffic circle to go northward on the road toward Tabarre. Dorven found himself in a foreign country, a stranger in his own country. At the cross roads of Claircine, a Shell gas station with a shop served the entire region. Just across the street to the left was a small park where some guys were seated under a tree to enjoy the shade. The jeep went east on the "Boulevard 15 Octobre" until the former president foundation. A monument of galleon, an old slave ship, divided the traffic on the boulevard in front of the foundation.

- It's been a long time you were in the country sir, the driver asked?

- Twenty-five years.

- Ah yes! One quarter of a century.

- I was sixteen years old when I left the country.

- Go more slowly, suggested the other employee, it will let him see the countryside and get reacquainted with his country.

The car went slowly to reach a long beige hedge.

- That is the private house of the former president, indicated the driver. It is very beautiful, a small mansion with large grounds.

The car continued slowly along the right as other drivers were speeding by on the modern highway. Heavy dump trucks were loaded with sand, rocks or gravel. A Hyundai dealer was on the left. From there we can perceive in escape line, according to a tiny distant view," Belleville", a small romantic town, of European style, in a spectacular architectural design. Avoiding the main road, a short cut led them to Pétion-Ville. The car went along the fence of the cemetery, continued around the flea market.

- Mister, you say you left the country at sixteen, the driver asked?

- Yes.

- Did you know this city?

- To tell you the truth, no.

- It's Pétion-Ville, an old bourgeois city, perched on the mountain with old houses, but clean and decent. It was built in 1831 by the former president Jean Pierre Boyer. In the past, when we spoke of Pétion-Ville, we imagined a noble magic city in the French tradition. We could see some wonderful small mansions. Now everything seems upside down. Things go wrong.

- Ah yes! This is unfortunate, frankly. How do you explain this deterioration?

-Well Sir, poor people, who dream of becoming bourgeois, invades the city, but they can't afford to live here, and the bourgeois gradually moved away. So you can understand that humble people, helped by angry politicians, turned it into the kind of slum that you see.

- Ah! It's really sad to see it.

The jeep climbed the ramp through Pan American Street, moving smoothly on the road.

- Have you left your family abroad, the other guy questioned?

Dorven felt uncomfortable, but tried to come up with an answer.

- So… yes I live alone.

The jeep crawled up the mountain of Laboule. The road was a long dark grey band drawn on the top of the green, still flooded in sunshine. Laboule, Fermate, Thomassin, Kenskoff villages appeared in a row. The car stopped near an architecturally modern gate. Some flowers, red, white and purple, spread along a fence of massive stones. The other employee got off of the car and pulled a bunch of keys out of his pocket. He opened the sliding gate and the driver moved slowly in. The courtyard was full of trees. Lights were attached to each gate pole. A short fir tree had been trimmed to be round. On both sides were medium-sized coconut trees. On the right near the fence a huge fig tree stood straight and vigorous, as if were a sentry that had watched the whole estate for years. In the backyard was a tall oak looking as if it were touching the blue vault. Flowers such as fire of paradise, orchids and red roses spread their colors. Inside, in leafy, greenish shade, the house seemed to overhang the whole bed of flowers.

- Oh! The stranger exclaimed, this is a paradise, a real paradise.

The two employees were busy unloading the jeep.

CHAPTER VII

The Chapel of Saint Gerard chimed seven. The family members were all in the living room, waiting for news. A heavy fog spread over the entire city, intensified by the dark night. Father Beaujour had just come back in. Mother got up, disappointed, and her face expressed enough frustration for a century, one could say. The others followed her one by one, some toward a room, and some toward the porch. The maid hurried to provide light someway, somehow. The voice of a candle seller broke through the night, crying out his goods. The blackout, a perennial challenge, was frustrating. No one will ever get accustomed to it. Unexpectedly Adélina's cell sounded like a horn, three times.

- Hello, she said.

- Hello Adélina? Said an unfamiliar voice.

- Who wants to speak to her?

- Dorven. Tell her it's the guy she met at the airport this afternoon.

- Oh, Dorven! I'm surprised. I didn't expect you to call me so quickly.

- It was a promise, you know.

- Oh yes, I know.

- I'm calling to give you my phone number.

- Just a moment, let me get a piece of paper...now go ahead.

- 586-1919.

- What?

The voice repeats the number.

- Very well, I have it now. How was the trip from the airport to your house?

- Very good, thank you. It seems you were worried about me.

- As you probably know, nobody is safe in this country with this cruel and insecure climate these days, so the fear could be worse for a diaspora just landed.

- Well! In fact, it was wonderful, my trip. Both guys who came to pick me up did an excellent job. It didn't take too long to become friends. They remained quiet a moment.

- Now tell me, Adélina.

- What?

- Where could I meet you?

- I don't know. You... you can still come over to my house if you wish.

- Now, if possible.

- How could you? You must come yourself? Can you get here alone?

- One of my friends could drive me over.

- No Dorven, take your time; it's unsafe. It's better to come tomorrow. I am sorry after tomorrow. It's would be better.

- What a shame!

- I am sorry, but you must wait. Excuse me Dorven; my phone will be dead in a few seconds. I have to leave you. Don't be angry, okay?

- That's okay Adélina, it's not your fault, I understand, Good night.

- Good night to you too.

Dorven hung up and continued to explore his new home. He has found it very compatible with his taste— gorgeous and luxurious, as fine as any residence on the French Riviera or in Venice. An architect-designer had decorated the mansion with the best furniture and lighting fixtures. A copy of a surrealist painting by JR Gérôme hung on a white wall by the front entrance. A little later a man and two women were introduced to him as his servants. The man started his job right away. Michel was blowing the horn, so he rushed to open the gate. The car lights illuminated up the courtyard and foliage. The moon was shining down its silver rays. The three servants squatted near the door.

- Come guys, follow me. Holding the door, Michel told them to enter. With caution they crossed the doorway.

- These people will work here, Sir. Give your names, guys.

- Alice, said one of the women.

- Elmise, said the other.

- Haristhène, the man said, a little shy; they call me Thène, cracking his fingers with a little smile.

In response Dorven just nodded, didn't even say his name.

- Excuse me Mr. Dorven, said Michel, I am going to show them the house.

- When you finish, come see me before leaving.

- Yes sir, I hear you.

Though Michel did his job for free for his employer, he was more than happy to stay with this generous man. This afternoon he gave one hundred dollars to him and his colleague Marc Andre.

Michel was showing the women what to do inside the house. After showing Thène around the courtyard and garden, he took them to their quarters. The two women will share a room, and the man has his own.

He joined Dorven in the living room.

- Yes, here I am back Mr. Dorven.

Dorven checked his watch—11:50.

- Is it too late Michel?

- Too late to do what?

- To take me out, fool, somewhere.

- Take you out somewhere! At this time! He was surprised. Ah, it is too soon for you to understand what's going on in this country. Anyway, Mr. Dorven, here people don't go out at night anymore. Even day time is risky.

- Another thing Michel. Suddenly he stopped.

- What Sir?

- Can you help me?

- How?

- I need girls, plenty of girls, beautiful girls.

Michel felt he was going to explode with a loud laugh, but tried to keep a serious tone.

- I promise you, this won't be difficult, I think. Now it's night and I must leave you sir. They shook hands…

CHAPTER VIII

Marc André and Michel didn't take long to speak about Dorven when they met the next day at the agency.

- Michel, I suppose everything went smoothly for you after I left yesterday.

- I went home after midnight.

- After midnight! You must be superhuman. I didn't know you were so brave, believe me.

- At last! He took a deep breath. I really had to take care of this guy. He is a foreigner, ignorant of everything in the country.

They were near the office counter. The secretary, who was busy working, pretended to hear nothing. A few customers sat in the large waiting room.

- Marc André, guess what.

- What?

- He asked me to bring him girls, many girls, he said whispering.

- What? He laughed. It won't be difficult anyway. He has money and he's handsome. He has all that's necessary to get a harem today if he wants.

The secretary was smiling while stapling some papers.

-Well, to be honest with you my friend, I don't know where he gets that kind of money, that Dorven.

- What are you talking about? Didn't you hear? He spent twenty-five years in New York City.

- Obviously he spent twenty-five years there, but what kind of job was he doing to earn all that money? What does he do?

- We don't know, you and I, but if we trust what people say, anything is possible in that country.

- Not by working, anyway. On this earth, no workers get rich, not even a single one.

The secretary leered at them.

- Another thing Marc André, as they left through the main door, after much thinking last night, I came to a conclusion. Are you listening?

- Yes I am. Talk Michel, talk.

- The man is very rich, and at the same time apparently very generous with girls.

- I had noticed the same thing. So what?

- I'm thinking of setting Sabine up with him.

- Setting Sabine up? I don't understand.

- Listen Marc André, Sabine's father, this poor man, who spent his life in the factory can do nothing now. You and I, we can do nothing either, we can only share their bitterness with them. As their best friends, we're witnessing this family's hardship after the loss of their two sons, killed and riddled with bullets by cowards. Right after the funerals, the old man was in financial trouble.

- I hear you Michel, and I understand your point. However, to set up Sabine— I don't see how you will succeed. She is not the type of girl to play prostitute. I understand your desire to help this family, but to hurt the girl is unforgivable.

- We must try. Who knows? Sometimes one uses the bad to do good....

- This will not be easy at all. Sabine is not the type of girl who will do it, I am certain of that.

- Somehow I will try.

Following Adélina's directions, Dorven slowly drove his brand-new BMW X5 from Furcy to Carrefour Feuille. They kept in touch during the trip by phone. As usual, near the sanatorium the streets were crowded with workers and merchants returning home tired after a hard day. Around the corner near a big stone, not too far from a huge pile of garbage, the chip-shop woman was busy frying food. Two customers were waiting with impatience. A soccer ball, kicked by a powerful shooter, almost overturned the kitchen fryer. Adélina's eyes were riveted at the crossroads. A wreck of a car was struggling to climb a hill, rumbling while its muffler spewed a blackish trail of carbon dioxide and the smell of gas.

It was like a theater curtain rising on a great show when the shiny gray jeep pulled over next to Adélina. The rays of sunset that filtered through the tree leaves on the west matched the silvery brilliance of the car. The soccer game stopped. The chip-shop woman stopped peeling, frying and cooking. She went into the crowd, lifting her head. A hungry dog near the shop stole a piece of meat and ran away. The woman grabbed a stone, threw it furiously after the animal, which yelped. Some curious onlookers riveted their eyes on the scene, as if amazed that Adélina would introduce such a great person to this neighborhood.

Hand in hand, Adélina and her guest walked over a ruined road down a slippery slope, across a wood culvert casually laid over a gully, then climbed up the other side through the cluster of squalid shacks. They reached a dead end by a wall with a bread-fruit tree. Finally, it was her house: old with dark blue walls with wrought iron rods, painted off-white around the entire veranda. They walked slowly and spoke while smiling. Three steps led to the porch through an old wrought iron door.

- Here we are Dorven, I'm home. Our house is a modest one. I am the youngest of a family of five. We are all here. We only know this neighborhood and house. We may be poor, my family and I, but we rely on two essential things: our honesty and our morals, which make us proud of ourselves.

- What about your beauty Adélina? This is a real asset you must be proud of also. You could be the muse of inspiration for any artist, poet or novelist.

- My beauty, yes. Beauty is always fascinating, but also fragile and ephemeral like a flower, depending on who bears it.

They were still standing on the gallery. Opening the main door of the house, she led him into the living room and made him sit on a mahogany sofa cushioned with plastic.

- Wait a little while; she said deliberately, let me bring my parents.

She returned with the old couple. Then, smiling she says

- Dorven, here're my mom and my dad.

He hastened to stand up and greeted them.

- I am Dorven Marc Forest.

Both parents sat down on the love seat, beside each other, while Adélina was close to Dorven.

- Are you from Port-Au-Prince, Mr. Dorven? The old man asks.

- Yes sir, Port-au-Prince.

- From which family?

- The Marc Forest family.

- Marc Forest? I remember having heard this name somewhere, he says, searching his memory. But... pardon me, I can't remember really. You know, at my age, memory doesn't serve me well. They remained quiet for some time.

- Do you live here or elsewhere?

- I have just returned to the country, ten days ago. I spent twenty-five years in the U.S.

- Obviously you left the country very young.

- Ah yes Mr. Beaujour, I was sixteen years old.

- Yes of course, you spent a quarter of a century there; this is a lifetime.

- Of course, he responds with a shy smile.

- You're on vacation? I suppose you will go back soon to resume work.

- This might be surprising to you; I won't go back there. After all these years abroad, I have decided to return and live in my country for the rest of my life.

- Since you ran away, how many times have you come home?

- Five times, the last was for the funeral of my two brothers killed by shooting

- Two brothers killed at the same time? They were shocked.

- With one fell swoop.

- Oô! Our deep sympathy to you Mr. Dorven, they implored.

- Thank you!

- Your father and mother, are they both alive? Where are they?

- Before I left the country, we lived in Bel-Air. My dad and mom passed away, not too long ago. We are now four brothers and sister.

- Ah! You might be suffering a lot, poor guy. The mother was looking with wide eyes, shaking her head with deep compassion. Adélina looked sad. She felt very confused, because the man had told her that he returned for the first time in twenty-five years out of the country. Not once did he mention a death in his family.

Sending a brief glance at her daughter and then turning his eyes to his wife.

- Well, in short, Mr. Marc Forest, what are you doing for a living? The father's conversation with the diaspora recently landed at Toussaint Louverture Airport seemed to take on another dimension. And he began to feel embarrassed, not knowing what to answer. One reply could silence this question of a rich man who landed in this miserable area with his millions. But it would be too impolite and arrogant to do it that way. He rather replied:

- It's a long story, Mr. Beaujour.

- You know Mr. Marc Forest, you might find me a little curious, but we live in a confusing situation in the country these days. We should know with whom we are dealing.

- Ah! It's really chaotic and confusing, the mother interjected, grimacing.

- Sometimes you wonder how things are going to go, explains Mr. Beaujour. Nobody knows the future. Here, nobody knows who is who, what is what.

- On my first minute in this house, I can tell that you are a very modest and respectful family. You won't be deceived Mr. Beaujour; I will behave, trust me.

Then the mother, Madeleine Beauvoir, wanting to end the awkward conversation between her husband and the stranger, decided to intervene.

- My husband is a troubled man, who has seen too much in his lifetime. That may be difficult for you, but it could not be otherwise. We were pleased to meet you today. Now we leave you with Adélina. Good night!

Driving back on the same route, Dorven was the object of everyone's curiosity. It was a quiet scene, but people stood on both sides of the road with eyes opened wide. The whole neighborhood had been aware that he was inside Adélina's house. Everyone had something to say. A lot of speculation took place: some argued said Dorven is a minister, the head of the government; others said he was a senator in the last legislature, very rich – perhaps a bourgeois comprador, who was living in the marquis after being a victim of the abused people, the exploited ones, the proletarians – finally a notorious traditional bourgeois, involved in a smuggling narcotic deal.

CHAPTER IX

After three months of sexual adventures, the damage caused by the madman was enormous and disastrous. It was as if planned, the gust that carried away all the pretty girls to death. Haiti, a third world country, is very vulnerable to the dread disease, given its poverty and needs. Young people are always exploitable and so exposed to the fatal disease. The devil man doesn't care about the young people; he acts like a monster launching a war against a nation.

Near the house by the gate, the horn honked four times. Thène hastened to open the gate. The driver, a little old man with a grayish frizzy beard, his face lit by his bright eyes, crossed the entrance slowly. A couple was sitting in the back seat and talking about everything, but nothing really. That was Michel with Sabine. They both got out. The driver parked the jeep before heading to Thène. They got into a verbal dispute about winning lottery numbers. Sabine followed Michel toward the front door. Thène noticed her physical resemblance to the boss, but said nothing about it. *Je wè, bouch pe, [see something, shut up],* his grandmother often said or *mache pye w rete bouch ou [walking with your mouth shut up].*

The girl waited in the living room. Michel went to Dorven's room to announce this rare beauty. She was dazzled, impressed by this bourgeois village, which she never visited. It was like a fairy tale inside the house.

The men approached her one after the other. She couldn't control her emotions, because of the physical effect the stranger had on her.

- Sabine, said Michel smiling, this is my friend Dorven. He is a friend I met a few months ago. You can trust him. He is a gentleman. You might think it wrong to introduce you to a friend just like that, a stranger, but everything is cool.

- I am Dorven, he said holding out his hand, smiling.

- Good evening sir, standing and holding out her hand as well, I am Sabine.

She felt strange and became more and more quiet.

- I think Sabine is very delightful, complimenting her, but very shy at the same time.

-True or false, says Michel, what is your response Sabine?

- True, I realize it. I can do nothing about it. It's innate.

- Wait a moment, said Dorven.

He went to the intercom to call Alice. The woman came into the room, her head wrapped up in white madras; an apron of the same color covered her from chest to knees.

- Please bring us some beverages Alice. What do you want Michel?

- Some cold rum.

- And you Sabine?

- A white wine, not much.

Now, with beverages served in the dining room, a conversation began.

- Sabine and I have been friends over the years. As a matter of fact, I am a friend to the whole family.

- That's fine, said Dorven, perfect. The three talked, talked, talked endlessly while drinking.

- I was hoping you would stay here Sabine, suggested Michel. I will be with Oblijan. I'm not going too far from here; I have to take care of some business.

- So you leave me here with your unknown friend.

- Unknown yes, but a decent gentleman, morally speaking. Don't be afraid—relax. He is my friend, he said smiling as he left.

Outside, the engine was running. The tires pounded the rough road.

Dorven took a little sip of rum.

- Are you familiar with Furcy?

- No, why?

- Nothing at all, I am just curious. They remained quiet for a while. Not too far away, there is a garden you might enjoy.

Leaving the drinks on the dining room table, Sabine's glass half full, they went to the front door. Just before exiting, the man adjusted his sunglasses. They were about to pass through the gate when they met two peasants, who greeted them and said a few words.

- They are brother and sister said one, there is no doubt. Their resemblance is very remarkable.

Maybe they are twins, said the other one.

- Do you hear Sabine?

- Yes, I do.

- What do you think?

- It happens that some people look alike. I didn't realize it. When we return home, I'll take a closer look in the mirror to see.

- I don't think so. You and I can't look alike.

- Why?

- Because you're too pretty.

- You also, you are handsome.

- Really? Thank you.

The midday was relatively warm. The leaves were shining under the hot sun and they trembled, caressed by a little breeze. A flock of black birds were flying, stretching their wings in the air. Right next to the car was a rider on a horse; the horse's hooves reverberated on the hard road. At five hundred meters from the house, they turned to a twisting road and drove through a field. Some tall trees and large branches shaded the area. Dorven and Sabine stayed under the foliage, by a brown rock with a floral roof near a hut made of massive uncut stones, just like a cave. A sweet smell of eucalyptus was floating everywhere in the air. They sat down on the rock.

- Will you forgive me Sabine?

- Forgive you, for what?

- Something happened to me that I must tell you about. Are you listening?

- Yes, go ahead.

- For the first time, I've fallen in love with someone.

- Who then?

- You.

- Really! See, that's great, but bizarre. Do you also want to forgive me?

- Of course, but for what? Your love?

- Oh no, what a funny idea? Pardon my memory... I forget your name.

- Dorven.

- This is not your full name anyway.

- Dorven Marc Forest.

- Marc Forest?

- Marc Forest Yes, why?

- Are you serious? After a short pause she said, I never heard of anyone else with this name, except for a few of my cousins.

- What are you talking about Sabine? Are you also Marc Forest?

- Of course Dorven, my full name is Sabine Marc Forest.

- It's really curious. By the way, where are you living?

- In Bel-Air

They remained speechless a few moments. Dorven began to think. He thought about his childhood in his old neighborhood.

- Bel-Air is really big, I know.

- Just to be exact, I live on Rouille Street, adjoining the Chapel of Our Lady of Perpetual Help.

- This is exactly my spot, he thought, without revealing anything to the girl. To be certain, he asks another question, the last one.

- What is your father's name?

- Germain Marc Forest.

Dorven changed abruptly. Looking at her, embarrassed, he stopped talking, as a Haitian proverb says: *chat pran Lang li [keep quiet]*. He scratched his head and became cold. He felt so strange and weak that a leaf could blow him over. He began to focus on the physical features of the girl: the shape of her forehead, her eyebrows, and her eyes with this strange gleam, her neck, the shape of her mouth, so cute, her noticeable aquiline nose, cheeks with smooth skin, her height and her swinging gait. She has a sarcastic tone when she laughs. She could be his exact double. He came to. She is my sister, he said to himself. Oh boy!

- I love you Sabine.

- You told me. I love you too. We are both Marc Forest. We are the only family in the country. We are not a large family. No doubt we are related.

- I have the same feeling.

Then his head was full of ideas. As in a movie, scene by scene, his whole childhood flashed before him. He thought about going to his family, to regain faith, beg their forgiveness, but it was too late because he knows his father, that difficult old man. He is perhaps worse than before. He kept his secret to himself.

- How do you find my place Sabine?

- Admirable, superb, especially with these plums all along the fence. I am only afraid of this hut; perhaps dangerous animals could hide there.

- Laughing with her, he said, you're right. They told me that a former owner of this place, a plantation owner during slavery, wanted wolves on his land and brought a couple from Europe. Because the species is carnivorous they are always hungry. One day, the wolves were howling everywhere. They sent some slaves after the wolves but they devoured them all. They were full for hours. A slave sorcerer passing by changed them into two women. Since then there have been witches in Haiti.

Sabine couldn't stop laughing.

- Now let's go back Sabine. I hope that Michel is already there. He'll take you home, up to Bel-Air.

CHAPTER X

The many steps in getting a U.S. visa for her husband were done so quickly that Marie Lyn managed a trip to Port-Au-Prince with John to the American consulate. Their first night of love had been a catastrophe, which could bring the authenticity of their union into question as far as the Immigration Service was concerned. Their case officer will be very tough.

Mary Lyn had changed significantly since her first meeting with John. She had surrendered willingly to the man (Dorven) who had no respect for her, who degraded her to the lowest level. She felt devastated by guilt that tormented her soul, troubled her conscience. He took her virginity, and in return gave her a check for five thousand dollars, which she refused. Her virginity was supposed to belong to her husband. She has paid dearly for her craziness. She has lost her pride, her essence. She feels she is no longer the woman she used to be. She can't apologize to John. She feels guilty for her behavior.

At Toussaint Louverture International Airport, John and his cousin were on time to greet Marie Lyn. It was crowded with people waiting, and there were some strange and suspicious characters in the crowd. Anyway, everything was all right, and they returned home safe and sound. Those cowards in New York, who had warned her of the chaotic situation in the country, are too secure. They doubt she will be able to come back. Maybe she doesn't care; she always thinks that the bad news coming from Haiti is a tactic to scare the tourist industry. The cruel insecurity is caused by invisible hands that make the country unstable. Those invisible hands are everywhere: in the parliament, police and judicial system. A cousin tells her that she is excited to get away from the misery in Haiti, a pongongon [shackle] to make her go through in U.S the fourteen stations of penance.

- I don't care either way. I don't and won't ever beg anyone for help.

A violent argument took place between the couple in their bed; their late honeymoon.
- I am beyond frustrated Marie Lyn.
- Why so John?
- You ask me why?
- Yes, what's wrong? I ask you a simple question.
- Do you imagine how much I wanted your love when you left me the last time without even a kiss? What kind of wife do I have? Are we really married or not?
- Well, I have come back in less than six months.
- To confess your sin or because you love me?

- I don't know. I was thinking a lot about you. You're my real husband.

- Do you have a fake one too?

- No, it's just a term to make husband sound stronger.

- Oh! Please! Why so much philosophy? What a happy and a lucky husband I am.

- I am anxious. I wanted to please you as a wife. Despite the risks I took to come to you, I am still bad in your eyes. You don't show any sign of comprehension or affection. What else could I do, please tell me, tell me please, oh God!

- Let me tell you the truth Marie Lyn. I am intelligent enough to understand your tricks and all the crap in your fabulous story. Do you think that I am a fool or the last of the imbeciles? Why suddenly do you try to treat me in such a special way when you left me without any show of love after our wedding? For five months you didn't show any concern for me, not even a phone call to the husband you left very far away in Haiti. Do you have the nerve to apologize, make me believe your bullshit?

- Do you want to insult me John? You accuse me without evidence, without reason. Do you suspect me of being unfaithful to you? What kind of woman do you think I am— a sidewalk whore, a slut? Do you think I bought an expensive airplane ticket and left New York to come and hear those nasty words from you? Have you caught me with somebody cheating on you?

- Your behavior is evident; it confirms what you just said. Only idiots make sacrifices for women, the liars.

- You also are liars, bad guys who treat women like pigs.

- Maybe you have an idea of what you're talking about. You reveal your hidden secrets.

- Enough John, enough— if you don't want me to kill myself, she shouted, tears streaming down her face.

She turned her face toward the wall and hiccuped. Lying on the bed, she was so pretty, so fresh, so attractive. John was so glad to be the happy conqueror of a so beautiful woman, the most beautiful in the world. He admired her body, her hair scattered on the pillow. Her eyes, though misty with tears, kept their crystal brilliance. Her skin was as smooth as silk.

- I'm your wife first and foremost, she says again. Can I be certain you love me, despite all these unfounded accusations? She said blowing her nose. It's true I didn't do my duty, leaving you alone the last time. I was so foolish then. Why don't you forgive me? I admit my craziness and my mistakes.

John drew her to his chest, caressing her hair. She raised her head a little to stare with tender eyes at the man, and then snuggled up to him. He began to cuddle her. Suddenly it was like a burning ember exploded. Her whole body was swaying voluptuously; she couldn't stop groaning. She turned around, her face up and spread her legs. When John tried to get into her, it was as if he was possessed. He fought in vain to control himself. Marie Lyn was alarmed, looking at him so changed. She couldn't believe her eyes. His bulging eyes were red like two balls of flame and his hair was spiky. He became a devil or bewitched. He looked at the woman angrily.

- *Tonnè*, he screamed, *tonnè*! You are in danger guy, I'm telling you, danger!

He punched his chest three times with his fist; it's me
Katawoulo, the Guinea man, who is talking.

- I am here. Goddammit I am here. I've come from far
Very far from Guinea
I crossed clumps of brushwood
I crossed fire
my feet are safe.
He stood up, dancing on one foot and singing, swirling.
- My horse is my horse
Hey! Hey *fout*!
I'm not afraid of evil.
Hey! Hey *fout*! Death is threatening
Death is flying
Ghost becomes smoke
the horse is safe
Hey! Hey *fout*!
Evil diarrhea is an incurable illness
My horse is my horse
I'm not afraid of evil
Death is threatening
Death is flying
Ghost becomes smoke
the horse is safe
Evil illness,
Stay away from my horse
Stay where you belong
I'm leaving now.

Then suddenly he began sweating. He collapsed on the bed and fell deeply asleep. Frightened, Marie Lyn did not understand the message of the unknown god to the possessed man. There were words full of mystery that only a mediator between her and the spirit could interpret: Death is threatening, death is flying, ghost becomes smoke, the horse is safe, evil illness, stay away from my horse. The final sentence, "Stay where you belong" caught Marie Lyn's attention. He began his message with "danger" and was unable to have sex with her. When she returns to New York, she will see her physician because it seems urgent. She couldn't sleep and was terribly disturbed. The spirit that put John in a trance changed Marie Lyn's mood. She felt disappointed. She wanted to return to New York as soon as possible.

The night was too long. The roaring of the cars resounded in the darkness, a cock crowed from time to time, and an angry voice broke the silence. Heavy steps pounded the pavement. Dogs howled. A drunk stumbled here and there, rambling. It was four in the morning. Four in the morning in a drowsy town sunk in the dark. The sun will relieve the moon. So many people will resume daily work, struggling desperately for a living.

- Wake up, it's time. Four o'clock.

The sleeper rolled on his back, stretched his legs, and curled up, humming.

- John! She shook him strongly, John!

- Hum, he answered with a strangled voice, as if it were stuck in his throat.

- Hurry up, it's time.

He quickly jumped up, and then sat on the bed with a drowsy face.

- Get ready darling, we must line up at five.

- Have you already taken it, rubbing his eyes and his face roughly.

- What?

- Your shower.

- Of course, I am done. It's almost four-fifteen, hurry up. You're going to make me late.

Outside in the east, a purple glimmer fought against the darkness to overcome a mass of gray on the horizon. Vans were going under drizzling skies. Their car went slowly on the ramp toward Delmas 33, Delmas 31, Delmas 19, until Delmas 3. They turned left to Delmas 18.They found a good parking space near the Faculty of Law and Economics. They walked to the U.S. Consulate. It was almost five. They found a good seat because they were early. They did not wait long to be called inside. The secretary gave them a number, which was his horoscope number, twenty-three.

Some thirty minutes later.

- Number twenty-three, please step in, said a female voice. Wait for the security guard to escort you.

They got up, the woman holding her husband's arm, escorted by the security guard, and took fifteen steps to the window.

- You are madam, the officer asked.

- Mary Lyn C. Bèrouette.

- And you sir?

- John Henry Bèrouette.

- Who is the petitioner?

- I am sir, answered Marie Lyn in a serious tone.

- Tell your husband to leave the room. We must be alone.

- Are you going to call him in later?

- Sure, when I'm done with you.

The security guard took John about thirty meters away.

-You are Mrs..... said the officer very sternly.

- Marie Lyn C. Berouette.

Your maiden name, can you say it to me?

- Mary Lyn Carmie Brun.

- Your husband's name?

- John Henry Bèrouette.

- Could you tell me the date of your marriage?

- On the fourth of March, twenty...

- Were you married at church or registrar?

- At a registrar in Port-Au-Prince.

- Which?

- The Delmas one.

- Do you have children?

- No sir.

- You Mrs. Marie Lyn and Mr. John, is this the first marriage for each of you.

Yes sir.

- You are here with your husband, but you were not obligated to come.

- I know, but I wanted to accompany him, sir.

- How long have you been in Port-Au Prince?

- Just yesterday.

- When you came back yesterday had you seen your husband?

- He came to pick me up at the airport.
- Where were you last night— at a hotel?
- We were home at Delmas 65.
- Did you share a single bed last night?
- Yes.
- Did you have sex?
- No.
- How long has it been since you've seen your husband?
- It's been almost six months.

-A couple who have not seen each other and made love for six months, it's really bizarre. What happened exactly?

- I missed my husband. We both wanted to enjoy sex. We had a fairly long conversation before caressing. He was about to enter me when he was ridden by a spirit.

-By what? Asked the immigration agent with wide eyes.

- A spirit sir, an unknown god, something like that. He couldn't do anything; he fell asleep until this morning.

- Are you telling me the truth Mrs. Marie Lyn?

- Yes sir, why should I lie to you?

The officer was stupefied a moment, shaking his head.

-Go sit lady.

He asked the security guard to escort John back to him.

- Mr. John, did you have sex with your wife last night?
- No sir.
- How long has it been since you've seen each other?
- About six months.
- Why didn't you have sex? Explain to me.

- To tell you the truth, it's not easy to explain. Last night my wife and I were caressing each other before making love; exchanging a taste of honey while erect, I was suddenly carried away by a profound sleep. I only woke up this morning.

After those probing questions and many others, the officer asked the guard to escort the married man to his seat.

On the way back, talking to each other:
- Oh! Said Marie Lyn, it was more complicated than I thought, and stressful. Thank God, this matter is over now, and I am happy that you'll be beside of me in US. I was in a bad situation, wondering how I was going to get out of it.
- I sincerely regret... would you like to go to the hotel, darling?
- Why John?
-As you know, the house is crowded with all kind of people, moving about. It's so crazy like that, uncomfortable.
- It's up to you my love, but to do what?
- Aren't you my wife dear? What could a woman and her husband do in the hotel room if not love?
Marie Lyn burst out laughing; her laugh let him see her mouth and 32 teeth.
- What about last night? Wasn't I your wife, yes or no?
- Something very strange indeed happened to me last night, but are we going to suffer daily the effects of a jealous spirit? Should I repudiate you, my wife because of the whims of a *loa*?
And then they headed to Pétion-Ville.

CHAPTER XI

Whenever Adélina met Dorven, her heart was light and felt radiant. It was as if for the first time. Their four-month love had become more and more interesting. One week spent alone was enough to worry her. She was excited when Oblijan phoned her that he was going to bring her to Furcy, to her lover's house. She hadn't had her period, and she was feeling strange and sick.

In the vast courtyard at Furcy, she hurried to get out of the jeep and went inside to Dorven's room, as usual. The engine noise woke Dorven up from a nap. Adélina leaned on his body and kissed him. He hugged her, got his hands into her blouse, fondling her breasts.

- They hurt me, my nipples, she complained.
- Soon, your period?
- My period? Never mind.
- What are you talking about Adélina? Are you sick?

- Sick! Yes. Among other things, tell me your lies to explain your absence. Eight days since I have heard from you. What's your explanation? Talk to me, come on.

- A businessman, a longtime friend was with me for a week. We were discussing business. I was the only one he could count on.

- During the whole week?

- As his best friend, I could not deny him my help, you know. Let's go back to your situation, he said with curiosity, are you sick really?

She took his hand, made it touch the lower part of her belly.

- I'm expecting a child.

- What, pregnant!

- Why this loud cry? You don't want a child? You don't want him because you don't love the mother? You don't want to marry her either?

- It's not what I'm talking about.

- So what the hell is it?

- How do you know you're pregnant?

- It's been days since I've felt sick. As you can see, my body is swelling. Very often I feel dizzy. If I eat I get sick to my stomach. The smell of coffee and eggs gives me nausea. From time to time I feel like my entire system is moving upside down. See; just take a look at my face, very pale because of vomiting. It's painful.

He suddenly looked anxious. Dorven is the type who never really likes anyone or any girl. He has now changed. For the first time of his life, two human beings make his heart vibrate: Adélina whose feelings led him to passion, and Sabine, his sister to whom he would give all his wealth, to compensate for his ingratitude to his parents. But unfortunately he is sick and doesn't expect to live long. Both of them, Adélina and the child will be HIV positive. Within four months, Dorven has infected many; morgues and tombs are waiting for dead bodies. Adélina, not really knowing the man she is in love with, wants to have this child. Father and child, two dear human beings, would complete her life.

- Dorven! She called.

- Hum! He said, turning his face.

- I'm telling you about my pregnancy, you just say "what" without saying another word.

He remained still silent, thinking profoundly. What a pity, he says in his heart, that she can't guess what I'm thinking about, ah....

- You know darling, she came back a little calmer, before saying anything to my parents, I need your word.

- My word, you will have it my love, but not today.

- Not today, she asked angrily? Will you abandon me with the baby or what?

-No, no way, I won't abandon you with the baby Adélina. I'm not like that. You've have just told me about this. Give me a chance to think about our situation. They are both pensive.

- This is important, he says in a conciliatory tone. There is no time to talk about other things.

- What then?

- I will take you to Thara's tonight.

- I'm so depressed, you know.

- Oblijan will drive you somewhere to shop. I would like you to look very good tonight. This will be an amazing evening, very lively.

- I hope my nausea and my vomiting will stop, so I can feel better. Otherwise, we won't be part of the party tonight.

Light from the half-full moon pierced the darkness and was reflected on the purple and white roses. In the west some wispy purple clouds were moving in the gloomy sky. A sweet breeze was caressing the treetops.

Dorven, already dressed for the evening, pulled out his cell phone.

- Hello darling! Said Adélina's sweet voice.

- I didn't think that you were going to be so long.

- Pardon me, my love. Do you know dear, the shop where I used to buy nice dresses was shut down? We lost time before finding another one, which is new, I suppose. I have found something very chic that you'll like. Are you angry?

- No dear, see. I was only impatient. Where are you now?

- At Pelerin.

- Have you eaten?

- No, not enough time. We were rushing too much.

- Okay, I am waiting for you.

- Be patient my love, we'll be with you very soon.

Oblijan steps on the gas to climb the mountain. Adélina, although she's the lover of a rich man and her lifestyle has changed, feels comfortable with the driver who has become a friend to her. He always calls her "Miss Adélina." She is also a good friend to the domestics Alice, Elmise and Thène.

For more than three months she didn't go to her job at the airport. Her parent's house at "Carrefour Feuille", a shantytown, was slowly repaired. She even planned to buy land in another area, less populated and more pleasant, to build a house for the whole family.

- Whew! Darling, I feel so tired and hungry at the same time. Where is Alice?

- Alice, she called.

- Yes miss, I'm coming right away.

- Bring me quickly something to eat. Do the same for Oblijan. We're hungry, both of us.

- Be careful Adélina, don't dirty yourself my dear; you are so pretty, congratulated Dorven.

- Thank you my love. I hunted to find an outfit suitable to your taste because you're so difficult, I know you.

The car went down the road, turning left to "Laboule 12" and continued past the Barbancourt distillery and avoided the Grenier Route until the gate and the path leading to Toto's house. Oblijan suddenly hit the brakes. He moved toward the club after clearing the security guard. Near the main gate, Adélina got out of the car, the door opened by the driver. She waited a moment and took her partner's arm. She admired the scene inside. The interior was like a movie theater. When she came in, it was as if the crowd became paralyzed. Her partner seemed proud. Eyes were glued on her while the man beside her had his hand around her back. She was such a beauty, a curiosity that caught everyone's attention. She wore an off-white gypsy skirt an orange blouse showing her half-naked torso, beige leather heels, and a pair of gold and diamond earrings, matching the other gleaming jewelry. Her hair spread over her neck and fell down her back. Her eyes sparkled. The sweet music in background, the sound of a singer filtered throughout the room and an outpouring of affection touched each soul with a sweet feeling. On the stage, musicians began tuning their instruments: sax, drums, cymbals and keyboard. The singer tested the microphone with "Nu look tonight." Many sophisticated people were there. Some sat at a table. Others were at the large bar placing orders. Suddenly the music exploded and so began the first dance. The ballroom was full and moving. Dorven stood up, extending his arm to his partner; they slipped through the crowd. Their bodies and souls joined together, their eyes closed as if the universe did not exist. It was if they were traveling far away in the distance of unfathomable space. After the first break they went back at their table. She suddenly saw a woman staring at her. Stunned for a moment, she then ran to her.

- Mirlène! She exclaims, hugging her.

- Ooh! The other says laughing, how are you my dear? You forget about us all. What's new?

- So far, so good, but nothing new.

- Everything goes well for you, I hope. I've heard everything. I've heard about you. There is my table. Follow me; I have to introduce you to David and my other friend.

- David this is Adélina, a co-worker at the airport.

- David.

- Adélina, extending her hand.

- Nice to meet you Adélina. This is our friend Leopold.
They exchanged greetings.

- See you next time, my dear friends, I must rejoin my fiancé.

- Your phone is the same, asked Mirlène?

- The same, dear. We have to talk, call me.

She ran back to Dorven at their table. Leopold was very impressed, carried away by Adélina's beauty while shaking her hand. He followed her from time to time in the dance hall, cautiously looking at her.

It was an evening of fun. Oblijan and Dorven took her home in the dark night.

Meanwhile, Alice, Elmise and Thène were taking advantage of their boss's absence to talk about his affair, but with discretion because "the walls have ears." Here when you have a job, whether or not well paid, you must take it seriously so you don't lose it for nonsense; it's something to care about, said one. The three were sitting under the big tree.

- Ah, my fellows, eye sees and mouth shut up; it's true, but between us it's cool, began Thène.

Elmise laughed, stood up, and then shook the bottom of her dress.

- Don't kill me guys, I can't laugh. What is it, Thène?

- So you pretend you neither see nor understand anything. You are a bunch of schemers, all of you.

- Listen, said Elmise, quick to speak, I have pity for Miss Adélina. She doesn't know what kind of situation she got herself in, indeed.

- Ah! Guys! Guys! Alice said with a finger on her lips.

- Listen to me Thène, said Elmise. Have you seen that little girl?

- Who was she then?

- The tiny black one. She was sitting alone on one of the chairs in the dining room. She was a child, between sixteen and seventeen— not old.

- There are so many people coming here, I cannot remember exactly, I'm telling you.

- It was last Friday, early in the afternoon.

- Oh, I see, Alice said, a shy one with a kid headscarf?

- Yes, that's her, affirmed Elmise.

- You are just talking; you don't know anything, said Thène. Let me tell you what happened Friday. The boss gave a check to Oblijan to cash. I was with him. They did not have enough money at the Pétion-Ville bank, so they referred us to the one near the airport. Oblijan helped him fill the envelopes, more than two dozen. Some had five hundred U.S. dollars— yes I must tell you that; I am not lying. Since Friday night, he has been entertaining girls, until Saturday night.

- Guys, where are we, Alice asked, worried?

- Only God knows, said Elmise.

- They lined up as if in front of a *borlette* bank [lottery shop], where everyone comes to buy numbers.

- Don't you have any other examples except the lottery? It's really funny to you. Guy, you have too much to do with money, be responsible. You enjoy yourself by making the '*borlette*' dealers richer, those millionaires, with that pittance you earn. You've never won at all.

- Leave me alone, woman. This is my money, not yours. Mind your business.

- Mind my business, the hell? I'm only telling you to be careful with that game, whether or not you're angry, that's your business.

- Stop bothering me please. I need nothing from you.

- Leave him alone Alice, said Elmise in a peaceful tone. It was so good to enjoy the gossip. You know him— irritable.

- I didn't say anything bad Elmise. I'm telling him to save money. I'm saying this for his own good.

- Thène, let's get it straight—to tell the truth, there is nothing wrong in what she said, returned Elmise. Peace, let's start again our story.

- You enjoy gossip, you, Thène said smiling.

- We all do, said Elmise. What about the envelopes filled with money?

- Each of the girls got one.

- Here is *le suivant* [next], as the late Coupe Cloue said Elmise replies.

- This Coupe Cloué was more than a king; he was a prophet who predicted a lot of things.

- *Antre, antre, le suivant, kiès ki te la anvan, antre.* [Next, coming, coming, who's first?] Alice was laughing, dancing.

- No Alice, we had rather say the next, explains Thène. This is a different set-up where every one is female, contrary to Coupe Cloue's males.

- Ah, right Alice, Elmise says laughing, Thène was a good student at Poyo School, and he is teaching you the right rules.

- When I saw the girls in the courtyard, I thought about my daughters, Thène says with a hand on his lips. I feel really sorry for them.

- There is plenty to be afraid of. You have only daughters, said Alice.

- Everyone has, except Elmise.

- Later it will be sad. Time will tell, Elmise said.

- I'm hungry, ladies. Stop your gossip. Is there anything to eat in the kitchen? I am hungry.

- Stop our gossip? Alice replied. Wasn't you the one who started it? Come, I have a little something in the kitchen; I'll get it for you. The three of them left.

CHAPTER XII

The day after her return from Furcy, Sabine began to explore every detail of her face. She realized the pronounced resemblance of the man to both, her and her mother. She ran.

- Mom, I need you.

- You need me Bibine? Talk to me my dear.

- I met someone two days ago.

- So what happened?

- I was with Michel, and we went to Furcy.

- To Furcy, to do what?

- Well! Mom, you know, there are places in this country that we should visit. Yes I went to Furcy Mom. He introduced me to one of his friends. He had to leave me in the house with him, by the way. A few minutes later, the man invited me to walk in his garden. On the way, we met two people who noticed our resemblance; they would have thought we were twins if it weren't for our age difference. His name is Dorven Marc Forest. What made me more curious was his resemblance to you too. I thought perhaps he could be your son who lived in the U.S., the one you always talked about.

- Are you serious Sabine? Don't you know your brother's name?

- Yes, Venord if I remember well, unless he changed his name to Dorven.

- I really don't know, said her mother skeptically. Bibine, what happened between you and the stranger? Tell me.

- Mom! Do you think something would happen with someone I met for the first time? No, absolutely! He was only talking and telling a lot of stories, like he loves me, things like that. Me, after hearing his name, I was very cautious. He was too, he didn't insist. He is very rich, Mom; you should see his house. It's like a fairytale mansion

- All I can say is to watch out. Have you talked to Michel since then?

- No.

- Why?

- We must see Michel. He could tell us more.

-Let me take care of this Sabine. Don't mention anything to your father, he is very difficult as you know, she advised her.

- No Mom. I'm not that stupid.

So Michel came without delay. The midday heat wave was intolerable; the woman asked a young grandson to bring her a chair out in the street, near the wall of the Chapel of Our

Lady of Perpetual Help. Some passersby and street vendors walked along the unpaved little street.

- Michel, she began, I need your help.

- I am at your service.

- I would like our talk to be in confidence. I want to avoid Germain. You know, Sabine told me something that puzzles me. It is about a man that you met, is this true?

- Yes it is, but it was by chance. She was with me; I had to see my friend. And they... they have a connection.

- Relax my boy, I know my daughter. I am not worried. Sabine told me about the resemblance of the stranger to her and to me in particular. The problem is that we have the same family name, Marc Forest. He is your friend, so I hope you will help me uncover the mystery.

- Really? I didn't pay attention to the name, you're probably right; there is a mystery we must find out about.

- How did you meet him? Tell me.

- He is a client of the agency that I work for, and I had to pick him up at the airport. I've provided him with great service. Because I treated him very well, he kept in touch with me and we became friendly. He was a generous customer, and he's really not a personal friend. I can't promise too much, but I'll do what I can. Don't worry.

- Michel!

- Yes?

- Are you aware of our oldest son who went to the U.S. twenty-five years ago?

- I have always heard about him, but vaguely.

- The way Sabine explains it makes me wonder and I am very curious, frankly. Do you know Michel, life is really bizarre, and anything can happen.

- I feel your concern Mrs. Marc Forest. You're a mother first. For twenty-five years you haven't seen your son, it's a long time. You could consider him the prodigal son you are ready to forgive. You don't forgive him because he deserves it, but just because you're his mother.

- You understand me perfectly Michel.

- I will do my best to find out, I swear.

- Thank you Michel! Thank you again. God will help you to do it. He will reward you on my behalf; I am a poor woman.

- Mr. Dorven?

- Yes Michel.

- Have you seen Sabine? How was your talk with her? You have said nothing to me about it. I hope everything was fine.

- You know Michel, after a deep breath, Sabine is an innocent and respectable girl. She deserves to be protected.

- Have you?

- Absolutely.

- Sometimes, something occurs by chance. Do you know Mr. Dorven that something has just occurred to me?

- Really! What then?

- I couldn't make the connection between you and Sabine as far as resemblance, though you're both Marc Forest. I have been a friend of that family for years through the two youngest brothers, my classmates, who have died, unfortunately. They are simple people, the Marc Forests, honest and respectful. Germain Marc Forest, sacred fighter for a living, a man of great courage, is intimidating. I wonder if there is not a connection between you and those people because they are not a large family, the Marc Forests. I would be happy if it were true.

- Michel, I want to tell you one thing.

- What is it sir?

- I'm just stupid. I admit being a scatter brain, and I acted like a madman. My parents are too good; they don't deserve such treatment from me.... Then he began to tell him his whole life story.

- Perhaps I'm foolish to tell you the story of my life and family, he says in a friendly tone, but sometimes it's necessary to free the mind from secret worries endured for a long time. That's the reason it's good to talk to someone.

- What do you intend to do sir?

- If I could get someone to reconnect me with my parents, it would be the greatest achievement of my life. This person would be a hero to me, given the situation. I can't go there alone. I don't see how they will forgive me, my poor parents.

- Ah, this is not an easy task. But I promise, I'm going to do my best to get you out of this shameful situation.

- I would say this is an impossible mission for you Michel. I know my father.

- Trust me. I will approach your mother. I admit it's not easy at all, but I'll try my best.

Michel believes he is on the right track. Without wasting any time, he went to Bel-Air. Mrs. Marc Forest, with her distressed heart, rushed to meet her emissary as he was about to step on the porch:

- How are you Michel? Perhaps I'm worried —your face is pale, did you lose the case?
- Mom! He burst out laughing; everything is settled.
- Wait Michel, we'd better go outside.

She changed her dress, and then started to walk with Michel.

- Mom! He burst out laughing again.
- I have talked to Sabine; she's also wondering what will happen.
- Dorven told me everything about his life.
- Michel, you spoke to whom?
- To your son Dorven.
- I have no son by that name.
- Don't worry about this funny name. His real name is Venord, your son. He changed his name when he became a U.S. citizen.
- My God! She exclaimed. It's too good to be true. It's like I'm dreaming, in another world. I can't believe it! Michel, are you sure it's my son?
- How would I know if he hadn't told me himself? He doesn't think that you will come to him. He also doesn't think the Marc Forest household will welcome him. He thinks he doesn't deserve your forgiveness and that you won't forgive him. Perhaps you have already decided.
- No Michel, there is a way of doing things. I will do it myself. Nobody can dare blame me for anything. I am a

mother and an adult. I had no hope of ever being with my son. Oh! I'll be so happy to see him before I die!

- Mom.

- Yes Michel.

- How are we going to do this? Tell me.

- Come pick me up anytime. Just let me know by phone at least two hours before.

Michel left Mrs. Marc Forest very excited, her prodigal son found.

As always, the silent woods watched the mansion majestically perched on the hill. The sunlight unfolded like magic sulfur. The hoarse crow of a nearby rooster joined the noise of the car by the gate. Like a drum roll, the call of a wood pigeon perched on the top of an oak alternated with the song of a nightingale coming from the undergrowth, and filled the air. Close to the mansion a woodpecker worked on a palm tree. Its beak, just like a steel burin, dug strongly the tree day and night to finish its partner's nest for the next laying season.

Alice and Elmise were busy doing their work. Thène opened the heavy metal door. Oblijan parked the jeep in its usual space. Inside, Dorven's heart was beating so fast that it almost stopped. His memory of his mother was faded, distorted by time and misery. He was waiting with his heart full of fear and guilt.

His old mother, accompanied by her delegate Michel, approached joyfully, her heart light with forgiveness. She has already dismissed her former charges against him. There is only one thing she focused on— her son. Looking around curiously, she moved slowly.

Dorven was distracted. He seemed not ready to face the scene. However, he had worked hard to face this reality today. The tension is at its height. He thought about Sabine, his beloved little sister; he would like her to be here with his mother. Finally, it was like a brass bell, releasing a range of loud sounds, was vibrating in his brain when the door opened to a spectacular scene. The two characters are lost in a long, deep look without speaking. Then they hugged each other tight as if they were a single person. The other people were amazed at the spectacle of the desperate mother and the prodigal son.

CHAPTER XIII

Adélina thought a thousand times about how to broach her pregnancy with her parents, particularly now that she was showing. It was embarrassing, really. She had never managed to tell them. She realized that the surest way to placate her irascible parents was to have Dorven's words. She hardly tried the first time. She decided to surprise him at his house and come to a conclusion. It was a late Friday afternoon. There was no rain in the forecast, but the weather was gloomy with blustery gray and wet clouds in the bleak sky. The sun tried somehow to pierce through with weak rays. Adélina walked along the street, said hello to Sissie, the chip-shop woman, whom she had known since childhood. She exchanged some words with a neighborhood friend before calling a taxi. She got in and waved goodbye to her friends.

Usually, the little door next to the big gate was kept locked, but by chance it was open. She pushed it and stepped inside.

The jeep wasn't in its parking space. Perhaps Dorven might be in his room and Oblijan out on some business for him. A wind that moved through the trees also floated up her white skirt and fanned her hair. The bird songs were still animated, and Adelina's ears thrilled to the sounds. The woodpecker continued work on the palm tree. Adélina went to see Elmise and Alice in the kitchen, and they joked a bit, and then she went into the bedroom. Dorven was not there. Even though it is a surprise visit to her man, she felt frustrated, considering the importance of her visit. She thought she could relax for a moment before calling Dorven on his cell, letting him know she was at his home. While stripping off her clothes and shoes near the big wardrobe, she saw a small plastic medicine bottle on the pedestal table, which caught her attention. She grabbed it and read the six characters AZT/3TC on the label.

- Oh! She exclaimed. What is it, AZT? Hum! I've heard about it, a medicine for the terrible disease AIDS.

She put the bottle back, finished undressing and lay on the bed. But she went back to the table, took the bottle and read it again. The drawers of one of the locked dressers were open. She pulled the drawers one by one, there were many drugs: Nelfinavir/lamivudine, Trimethoprim 160mg/ sulfamethoxazole, atovaquone/zidovudine, fluconazole 400mg, methadone, Rithonavir/zidovudine, valporic acid 500mg.

- Oh! Is this a pharmacy? You'd have to be seriously ill, near death to take all these drugs. It's really strange. She remained quiet a few moments and continued to look at the drugs. What's wrong with him, that Dorven? I don't know about those others, but this one, AZT/3TC, is a medicine for AIDS, I am sure of that. He is very likely infected, she said to herself. Suddenly many dark thoughts whirled in her brain. She began to collapse; it was like her soul was leaving her body. She closed her eyes and tried to stop the tears. She regained control of herself because she didn't want the servants women to notice her distress. She felt panicked, horrified, and then icy pain ran from her skull to her neck and down her spine to her heels. She wanted to scream, roar, a hunted animal brought down, crying for help. She saw herself in a fatal abyss of despair. What a terrible misfortune for her and her child! It was as if the world had collapsed in one fell swoop.

-Me, Adélina Beaujour, a victim of AIDS; me so reserved, so prudish and cautious? No, this is disgusting. I must die before I'm branded. What will my parents say? All my friends, she lamented in a whisper. Yes, that Dorven is sick, for sure. Why all that AZT? It's a medicine for AIDS, I am sure. I've heard about it, but to be sure, I'll see Dr. Pierrot. He can tell me.

She hurried to take a sample of each bottle, covered them in a handkerchief and went away.

The night was long, and it seemed like an eternity before the sun rose and she could finally go to Dr. Pierrot's clinic. It was Saturday morning, and she entered the half-open door to see the secretary.

- You've come here for the first time, madam, to see the doctor?

- Yes, but not as a patient. I need to see him urgently, it's important.

- The doctor sees only his patients today.

- I hope you don't decide for him.

- What are you talking about? Are you here to teach me how to do my job? Who are you? Listen lady, I don't know where you come from, but here I'm in charge, boss's orders. Are you a witch threatening me this morning? Go tell. Whoever sent you that you aren't powerful enough to get me.

- Listen to me, madam.

- Listen to what? She cried out.

- I'm not here for aggravation. I can understand you want to keep your job, but you are going too far now, nervous and upset for nothing. Don't you see how calm I am? Please announce me to Dr. Pierrot. He is the only one who can decide whether or not to see me.

The other patients commented on the situation and eventually intervened on behalf of the visitor.

- So, what's wrong with letting her see the doctor, asked one? Dr. Pierrot is a physician after all. You don't know why she is here. Think—you're a secretary, not a policewoman.

- If you can do the job better than I, come here to my desk, she replied. She was very mad at that woman. Then quickly as if she was about to explode, she went in the exam room.

- Doctor Pierrot, a woman is here for you, she acts like she will beat me up.

The doctor was examining a patient and did not answer immediately.

-Miola, I want you to know that you are not here to quarrel with my patients or visitors. You're my secretary. If you want the job, do it properly, with courtesy, or I fire you, understand?

- Yes doctor, she answered, like a child.

- What's the name of the person you were quarrelling with?

- I don't know.

- See. You only cause trouble.

She was polite when she returned to the waiting room, her hands joined as if in front of a confessional.

- What's your name madam?

- Adélina Beaujour.

- Thank you madam, I'll be right back.

She returned.

- Have a seat, madam. The doctor says to wait.

- Hey! hey! Exclaimed one of the patients who comments the fact, I told you, preventing conflict is better than begging for pardon.

- It's not their fault, says the other one. Some people are vile. They have no manners at all. They're like animals.

Adélina joined the doctor and received a warm welcome from her friend.

- Adélina, he approached her smiling and embraced her. All my apologies my dear friend, I am so sorry.

- Don't worry doctor. Forget about her.

- Do you know that my wife and I were talking about you yesterday?

- Really? What were you saying about me? I am here for an important matter Dr. Pierrot. I am in a big trouble; only you can help me. That's why I am here this morning. It's an emergency.

- In big trouble? Asked the doctor in his white shirt, his stethoscope around his neck. I will do anything, even the impossible, to help you out. What's the problem Adélina?

- You know, I have someone in my life; it's been five months since we've been in love. I found these drugs at his home yesterday. I would like you to identify them for me, please. She handed to the doctor the collection of drugs.

- AZT/3TC? He said, stupefied. He scrutinized the other drugs. All are medicines to treat AIDS patients. Did you have sex with him?

- Yes doctor.

- Do you remember how many times?

- Unable to say.

- You're not pregnant, I hope.

- Yes, I am.

- Ah, this is serious. Would you like an HIV test?
She shakes her head, yes.

- Wait a little while.

He came back and took her to a small room where he took a vial of blood.

- Listen to this Adélina. Keep your morale high and stay calm. Avoid thinking about your condition. Bad as it is, there is always a way out. It won't be the end of the world. There is always a chance because life is the key of destiny. Be strong my friend. Come back next Wednesday for the result.

- Thank you Dr. Pierrot.

The doctor's advice is comforting but not enough to prevent her from sinking into depression. It's a relentless burden on her and her child. She cannot avoid this. Pierrot is a doctor, the first to whom she confessed her secret.

-I don't know how to bring this up with Dorven. I would like to end all contact with him. How am I going to manage this bleak future? If the test confirms the virus, I'm already dead. I'm young and I want to live! I wasn't born to die so soon! I was careless, but when I asked him to wear a condom, he refused. He wanted to infect me! He is an evil man like no other, who hates people and uses sex to destroy lives.

The following Wednesday, her impatience came to an end. She did her best of to appear well so that no one could detect anything wrong. She went to the clinic. The secretary was extremely polite this time, tried several times to be friendly to her. She hoped her new friend did know anything about her situation.

- You won't wait too long, you're on time, she says, smiling.

- Thank you Miola, she answers with a serene glance. The secretary was about to launch into a topic when Dr. Pierrot showed up in the doorway. He smiled and called Adélina. She stood and walked to the exam room.

- How are you Adélina?

- I have followed your advice, she says smiling. I tried to keep up my appearance.

- You look very cute today, too cute. Did you sleep well?

- Not as before, but I slept.

- Undress and leave your blouse and slip on. I'll come right back. She was ready when the doctor returned.

- Lie down onto the table he said.

The doctor thought she was brave and controlled.

-Your blood pressure is normal and everything is good so far, no sign of concern. Okay Adélina. Get dressed.

They moved to the consultation office.

- Well, your health is the same, but the news is bad, painful. You are HIV positive.

Adélina is in distress. She begins shaking like a leaf. It's a death sentence. But she knows she must fight the virus to the end.

- Dr. Pierrot, I knew there was little chance I was safe.

- But there is a something in your favor. Your blood type is O positive. With your good attitude, you'll be in good shape. Keep your condition discreet, even with your family. Don't say anything yet to anybody.

- What about the child in my womb, will he be safe?

- Nothing can be certain in this case. He may or may not be infected. But as far as I know according to all scientific evidence, he has a 90% chance of being healthy and safe.

- How do you explain that?

- The child is protected from harmful microbes in his mother's womb by a sack. He is even protected against jolts by his mother. The most important point is, at this early stage, the child is already very remarkable. Although he is the genetic heir of his father and mother, he is different and unique…

- Oh Jehovah, she exclaimed, the first and last of the scientists! We are all the product of your sacred hands. You will save my child. Thank you!

CHAPTER XIV

Father Beaujour had endured considerable anxiety since his army pension was discontinued years ago. To him it was unfair and even shameful to put the burden of the family on Adelina's responsibility, a 23 year-old girl and the youngest. Sometimes the parents feel ashamed. Anyway, Adélina remained the column that supports this family. She couldn't afford to go beyond high school because she was taking care of the whole family, providing for them as a luggage handler at Toussaint Louverture International Airport.

For weeks she was unhappy. She kept a low profile. She bore her burden alone. She didn't sleep well because of nightmares; she was afraid of the silent dark. Her soul was sad, plunged into mourning, ready to die. She continued on with courage and kept her appearance up. In a short time they will no longer exist, she and her child, was the fear that traumatized her day and night. It's true she loved that man, as she never had anyone before. He brought a better life to her and her relatives with his generosity. But she wanted to get rid of that man. She didn't see him anymore. It's been more than a month. Suddenly her phone rang.

- Hello!

- Hello, said a female voice, is this Adélina?

- Yes. Who is this?

- Mirlène.

- Ooh, Mirlène! How are you, my dear? You didn't call me, why eh?

- I expected you to call me first.

- I don't have your phone number, do you remember?

- Didn't I give it to you?

- You have changed your number and we haven't spoken since.

- What's new Adélina? Tell me babe. The flower blossoms and becomes more beautiful?

- Yes, absolutely Mirlène, but we are going slow, you know.

- Do you know what Adélina? She laughed; are you alone, can I speak?

- I am alone in my room, without even a fly.

- I had to call you, but it took me time. I have news for you. Are you ready to listen?

- Oh yes, I am.

- Do you remember one of my friends you met at Thara's?

- Yes, I remember, but to tell you the truth, my picture of this guy is hazy.

- You might find me indiscrete or even stupid to tell you that. Leopold, the guy you met, has been driving me crazy, talking about you. He wants me to set up a meeting between you two. What a situation!

A silence between the two —no sound at all.

- I've lost contact, it seems. Are you still there Adélina?

- Yes, I am.

- You're saying nothing at all?

- No, absolutely nothing.

- Oh, Adélina, you know, he wants your number just to say hello.

- Ah yes, and why?

- Well, actually, you know, he can't tell me all of his feelings for you. He seems to be getting crazier about you.

- Mirlène I am sorry, I am going through a critical time; disaster is tormenting my life. I am not ready for a new relationship. See you, bye. I'll call you.

- When?

- One of these days.

- What should I tell him?

- Who?

- My friend Leopold.

- What I just told you.

Two days later, her mobile rang again.

- Hello, who is this?

- Mirlène, how are you Adélina?

- I'm doing great. I hope you forgot about what I said the other day, but I'm in a critical situation I can't control, I apologize.

- Don't worry dear, that's fine with me. By the way, do you feel better now?

- Yes, I try to be as usual.

- I saw Leopold, he asked me to give you his regards.

- Thank you, do the same to him.

- In fact, he's by my side; he would like to greet you himself.

- Oh, no thank you.

- Adélina! Adélina! Please be polite, my dear.

- Okay, let's go.

Leopold smiled before getting the phone. He felt his blood was flowing to his heart. Adélina, reluctant, heard the sweetness of the male voice in her ear.

- Good evening Adélina.

- Good evening sir, she replied indifferently.

- I am Leopold, as you know; I want to say thanks for accepting my greetings. I also want to congratulate you for being the angel I have never before seen. You are so fascinating, so beautiful that you are the first woman I've fallen in love with. My love for you is not a joke. You're the only one who penetrates my heart. When I touched your soft hand, I was so thrilled that I couldn't sleep. It was so delightful that it put me in a wonderful mood. Adélina, as you would a beggar, give alms and let me meet you at least once, just to enjoy a smile from your lips. I would be happy all my life.

There was not a single sound on the phone.

- Nobody at the end of the line, she probably hung up.

Then her voice was on the phone.

- I'm still here sir, listening.

- Thank you Adélina. I am sorry to keep you. This is not my fault. My heart suffers under the worst punishment. My soul is weak, lonely and desperate. In misery it's trying to cling to a sister, a partner who could banish its solitude.

Adélina, whose heart is tormented, didn't know what to say. The man was begging her.

- Why do you want to meet me? Can you tell me?

- To see you, or even to love you if you accept my worship. I am a damned soul who seeks a goddess. And here I am at your throne, offering my sacrifice. Please accept it, my goddess. Now I want to be at your feet to adore you, raise my heart to you and tell you of my suffering and my misery.

- You're begging too much.

- You deserve my supplication my goddess. I want to surrender, to be in your arms until death. Let me cry at your feet. Let me cross the threshold of your heart. I want to put your hand in mine.

- Your words are too flattering.

- I beg your love Adélina, if it's a damnation to implore you, condemn me so I will be trapped forever in your hell.

- Would you give me Mirlène?

- Are you done with me already? I'm not finished yet.

- I've had enough of your litany. You can't say everything today. Put Mirlène on the line, please.

- Mirlène, what his relationship to you, this Leopold. Is he your guardian angel?

- Not at all Adélina. I already have my angel, David, who watches over me day and night. Leopold, he wants to be yours. He implores you so much, huh!

- Well! What can I do Mirlène? Tell me.

- The key to your life Adélina is in your hands, your destiny. I'm just a bridge, not even a go-between; I don't want that role. You make a decision?

- What decision?

- Will you meet him?

- For sure I... I don't know yet. I... I think... I...I'll call you.

- Listen to me Adélina. You have talked with Leopold, right? He had a long conversation with you. Why are you changing your mind? Simply take his number and call him.

- Do you think it's easy to do?

- I didn't say that. We are no longer in the old world where the bride gets permission from her grandparents to kiss her groom before the honeymoon.

- What do you mean Mirlène? Someone I don't know, I only had a telephone conversation with; I cannot be comfortable with him yet. It's a matter of self-esteem, decency and morality.

- Adélina okay, okay, let's end it. I don't want you to get mad at me. Let him go to hell, let's remain friends.

- Give me his number Mirlène.

- I can't. He'll give it to you himself.

- Put him on the line.

Willingly, they exchanged numbers.

Attractive, dazzling, Adélina is a shining little flower. She is brown from the sun and the tropics and has ebony hair. In her dressing gown, she is svelte, slender like a goddess, a deity exhibited in a golden frame. Sitting between wreaths of flowers given by her lover, she seems sad. She is indeed adored by an obsessed man, who will probably get rid of her when he knows that she is an AIDS carrier. She is full of fear and doubt. "I see my happiness vanish behind a dark screen, she bemoans", she thought.

An opera aria begins in the evening. The voice sang soul fully through the speakers and sounded throughout. The music coursed through the room, through the flowers, through the girl's hair, sweetly filling her heart. The graduated notes of a piano played into the night. She heard the sound as a signal to depart. She could read the mind of the man and realized that his love was real, pure. It's a transparent and sincere love sealed with truth. This is love that travels far, very far, to the other side of memory. "Here is my happiness near me, but I can't take it", she continued to thinks. "It's forbidden to touch. Oh lost happiness, you come too late in my life. I see you hidden at the rear in a screen of darkness".

Suddenly, deep in melancholy, she sees a vision of autumn from another time, when the leaves are blown away beyond the clouds.

You are the season of my birth
The season of my childhood
Oh autumn
Eternal season that cradled me
You will die with my life
I will take you with me
To the bottom of my tomb

Then she remembered this verse by Guillaume Apollinaire:
Autumn is dead, remember
We will meet again on earth
A whiff of time, a strand of heather
And remember that, I am waiting.

She tried to hold off the shadows of sadness that drowned her joy and dimmed her beauty.

"Who can stop me from mourning my death too soon? Oh… I feel a hot and violent wind blow away my peace of mind. I feel my heart stabbed. My life is going gradually".

Then she plucked a petal, smelled its fragrance. She raised her head, with watery eyes.

- My age should give me some sense, she says full of remorse. Her eye lids were sticky and her lips puffy. Twenty-three years old, I am old enough to act accordingly. We are not dupes, we're not going for adventure; we're not going to misunderstand each other. You've lived in the U.S. for years.

- I beg you to believe me Adélina, I have no commitments, and I have no one in my life.

- I believe you. But you don't ask me anything, huh!

- Ask you what?

- The first time we met at Thara's, am I right?

- Of course.

- Moments after we met, I left the three of you to rejoin my partner at our table. Only two months after, here we are together, head to head like two lovers. Don't you think it's improper? You don't ask me anything, I don't say anything to you; maybe I am still tied up with him. Now, suppose that I become your lover, are you going to trust me? Will I be honest with you?

- I love you Adélina.

- You love me, I know. But we are not crazy. She paused and said, I'll tell you something and you'll be surprised Leopold.

- I'm listening my love, go ahead.

The opera continued. Some couples danced languorously as if asleep. Adélina swallowed a gulp of red wine.

- I love you, she said, smiling.

Leopold was stupefied, dazed. He couldn't believe his ears, what he heard from Adélina, a simple sentence, and words of hope, which he wanted so much to hear.

- I love you, she said again, but we need to talk and come to a clear understanding. Do you agree?

- Why not Adélina? I don't have a hidden life, something wrong that I conceal. My life is like a mirror, an open book where you can turn the pages and read as you want.

- I have a secret life.

- Ah yes?

- You are surprised? What did you expect? To tell you that I have a public life, which everyone…stranger or not has the right to know?

- Oh no Adélina, to the contrary. It is the strength of your expression that brings out my emotion. I fear the fragility of this love.

-You're right; our love is new, weak like a small tree branch that any breeze could break.

- Do you know Adélina? You may find me fantastic, stupid, ridiculous, absurd, raving, and obsessed, as you want, but I…

- Oh! Why all these scary words, you… what?

- I want to marry you.

- She burst out laughing. Oh! Marry me! What a wish and a strange proposal!

- Why are you laughing? I am not joking. Are you making fun of yourself? Is it because I love you to death? I'm crazy about you. I'll do anything for our love to succeed, whatever the sacrifices. I would be so lucky to have you as my wife. No woman is as charming, attractive as you. When I think that you must grow old and die one day, I wonder why death is so cruel and merciless. Life is unpredictable and cowardly; it doesn't defend its children.

- Don't say all this again, she says smiling.

- All my honors Miss Adelina. You deserve my flattery.

- Yes, it's written that everyone must grow old and die; you too, my handsome, she said calmly. It is a law no one can beat. She was pensive. You are going to make me think Léo.

- I agree. A life together is a serious commitment that we shouldn't take lightly.

- Are you sure?

- Yes, I am sure. I admit that I am running out of reasons.

- Just wait and see, Leopold. We have to be careful, both of us. You want to marry me. You take me by surprise. I need time to discuss this with my parents. It's a complicated matter, even difficult.

Then they talked softly until late that night.

CHAPTER XV

Sissie, the chip-shop vendor who has been in business for years in the slum, is the witness of numerous scenes. She starts working early in the morning, closes very late at night. She knows all the fauna of the environment: rascals, whores, dykes, witches, *"zenglendo,"* [thieves], kidnappers, honest people, poor people.... She is aware of everything. Every single detail of a situation, a story, is discussed in front of her shop. Balan, an itinerant bread vendor, is her companion in gossip to whom she explains everything, what's going on.

She interrupted a conversation she was having with a fellow gossiper on her cell.

- I'll call you later, she said to her.

- My fellow Sissie, says Balan, grabbing a small bench to sit down on.

- My fellow Balan, she answered, dropping the small device into her camisole pocket. I haven't caught up with you this morning.

- I passed by earlier. I wanted to be the first served this morning. I have three new clients.

- Not bad fellow Balan, not bad at all.

- I haven't had a chance to meet fellow Dor this week.

-He had, surprisingly, to work at "Vieux Bourg", and spent the whole week there. He has just returned.

- It's good my fellow. It's better than nothing.

- Do you want something fellow Balan? She said, circling her head to check in all directions, making sure there is no one around to hear her.

- Not now, thank you my fellow.

She gathered her camisole and sat down on the little bench beside Balan.

- I got news for you my fellow, she whispered.

- You make my heart warm, I can't wait to hear it, says the other, smiling.

- My fellow, making a cross with her index finger on her lips, I hope you keep it secret. I don't want get myself in any shit. I lived for twenty-three years in this neighborhood. All my children have grown here.

- My fellow, we were kids when we first knew each other. Since then we've been close, talking together. If you don't trust me these days, keep it to yourself.

- We have an apprentice kidnapper here. I've seen him.

- Don't say that. Kidnapper! Well, we are fashionable. Is it true what you're telling me my fellow?

- Well, a nasty dirty boy, a sneak thief. Poor people like us, how we can be kidnappers?

- My fellow, ooh hum! We are not connected to rich people for that kind of business.

- Yesterday evening, fellow Balan, I was with Zette, carrying my stuff. Just before crossing the culvert, I saw him disappear. He was suspicious.

- Who is this?

- I can't reveal his name, but you can guess, you're in the neighborhood. I didn't take long to return; Zette was following me. I saw him leaning against door of a jeep. He was talking with two strangers. I pretended I was cleaning and arranging my stuff. I went home, came back; they were still there. When I came back from my third trip, they were all gone. At four in the morning when I was leaving for the market, I met him coming back. I was hurrying, pretending that I knew nothing once more.

- Who my fellow, who? Tell me.

She grimaced. She put her mouth close to her friend's ear and whispered a name.

- My fellow, what are you telling me?

- As you hear my fellow.

She was silent while her friend considered the situation, shaking his head right to left. She got up, looked at her stove where vegetable soup was simmering. She came back and sat on the bench next to her friend.

- Now, let's change the subject. Things are strange under the blue sky, fellow Balan, twisting the bottom of her dress and putting it on her thighs.

The fellow came closer to her, bent his head to better hear the second topic. The gossiper looked all over the area. She got up again, went to the rear of the booth, and then sat down.

- My fellow, the beautiful gray jeep has disappeared like a flash of lightning.

- What, my fellow? With respect to fellow Dor and you, I want to pee.

- I'm killing you this afternoon, she blurted out.

- My fellow!

- Another has replaced it, a white car. The man, who dropped her off, never came out.

- Who is he?

- Well! Everyone has a version and maintains it, true or not. Some say he is Jean Jean Celeste's son with his mistress when he was poor. Because he is more responsible and honest than the others, they make him manage the estate. Others claim he is a Haitian millionaire's son who lived in France with his family. They have returned home, to the motherland. But someone who knows more of the story says that he is just a diaspora.

- They are so lucky; do you see their house my fellow?

- She has already bought a piece of land, and the house is under construction.

- Where?

- I don't know. Someone said that it's in an exclusive neighborhood. Putting her lips close to his ear, somebody told me she is pregnant. Now, don't accuse me of any gossip.

- What? Who's the father?

- I don't know; maybe the new one, maybe the old one, I know nothing. It's F.R.

- F.R my fellow?

- F.R, fire and replace.

- Ah, the dog is never too old to be rabid; do you remember that child my fellow?

- She was the best in the entire neighborhood.

- The most beautiful too.

- Pretty woman! Pretty woman! Let mine be just the way they are.

Suddenly, an explosion took place inside the booth with a thunderous noise, like a terrible bomb. Balan grabbed a bucket, filled it with water and doused the flames. He was horrified. Smoke spread all over and rose to the sky. Tongues of purple, yellow and red flames rose high. A crowd of people ran in the opposite direction, shouting for help. Some people hurried to call the fire department. Others, panicked, ran. The booth was buried in the ash; there was only the black debris of the burned pot. Both gossipers disappeared. The hot fire spread. Smoke continued to fill the streets, up to the roofs. The street was full of people, and the crowd was moving in all directions. Women cried out and kids were curious. The fire hit the crackling sheets. The heat was suffocating. Some thieves were running, pretending to offer help, but they really wanted to get into the houses, and the residents chased them off.

-See, an old woman shouted. See, how bad you are. The terrible fire is destroying us while you're trying to steal whatever is left, even our shreds of clothes. You're the real thieves' men. *Bann vòlò [bunch of thieves].*

In the middle of the slum devastated by the fire, two men were puffing, pulling out a sculpture of a muscular figure from a narrow doorway. Two others rushed to help. Together the four hauled and pushed. One arm of the statue was about to break when one shouted out.

- No guy, this side here, that side there, push the head upward. Now let me do the rest.

A puff of flame hit them at chest level; they pulled out the statue in the nick of time. They slowly carried it and placed it on the sidewalk. Its creator, torso soaked with sweat, was sitting nearby. It is the likeness of a forty year-old farmer with a straight torso, long neck, broad back and a muscular chest. The statue has a garden bag across his back and a sickle in his right hand. He is barefoot and his pants are rolled up to his knees.

- Victor! Ah, a man of courage—a great Negro. You have saved Leonord.

- My uncle, this work is my life. It's the first and last thing I had to save from the disaster.

A nice car drove slowly, toward the crowd. It stopped near the sculpture. The two men in the car, after looking at the catastrophe, turned their gaze. The passenger rolled down the window to contemplate the statue.

- What a masterpiece! He exclaimed to his friend, a talented artist. Can I meet the sculptor? Is he here?

Someone pointed him out.

- Are you the artist?

- Yes sir, why?

- Nice work, my congratulations to you. Are you selling it?

With a proud air, the sculptor crossed his arms on his chest and glanced at the man, who raised a cigarette to his lips, lit it and then exhaled the smoke. He was admiring the work while stroking his face with his finger.

- Did you hear me my friend? He asked, blowing out smoke. I am interested in buying your sculpture.

The old man turned his eyes to Victor and smiled.

- What are we doing? He asked Victor.

- Let's go in my car, said the buyer. What is your relationship to that old man?

- My uncle.

- I am Luc Fechner Dorélus.

- I am Victor, said the sculptor.

- I am Osmane.

- Tell me about the sculpture Victor.

- It is the likeness of my grandfather, a farmer who worked hard. He believed that we belong to the soil, where life begins. He always said that unity among brothers is the wealth of human beings. We must work together. We have to cultivate the land from generation to generation. Our living depends on it.

- These reflections perhaps inspired this classical work. I would like it to be mine.

- Why are you so interested?

- Your work has a lot to do with me Victor. I never expected to find a piece of art that would remind me so much of my father. It will be a memorial for me.

- Really! Victor exclaimed.

- You know, says the stranger, I am the product of the countryside. As the son of a peasant, agriculture made me who I am today. I would like to have this sculpture in memory of my father who labored on his land to make us, my brothers and sisters, special individuals. Your grandfather is the symbol of a courageous farmer.

Victor's eyes sought Osmane.

- What do you say uncle?

- Our sculpture is a work of great value, replied the old man with pride. It will depend on the offer.

- What's your offer Mr. Dorelus? Asked Victor to the businessman.

- One million.

- What?

- One million dollars U.S.

The old man put his hands on top of his head.

- Thank you Mr. Dorelus; let me get out, he said grabbing the door handle.

- Why my friends, why can't we make a deal?

- One million dollars is a ridiculous amount for my work, sir. By the way, the money will not be mine. It is to rebuild our slum devastated by the fire.

- A philanthropist, eh… a philanthropist is what you are? This money will be a drop in the bucket of that great project. What about one million and a half to make you laugh?

Victor and the old man agreed the deal.

CHAPTER XVI

The day after the fire Dorven wanted to see Adelina and went with his driver and servants to the disaster scene. He and Oblijan found a footpath to the ruins of the house. There was nothing there except charred debris and piles of rubble. They had to turn back without finding any of the Beaujour family or information about them.

They all took refuge in a hotel and were trying to rent a house. She will exploit this calamity as an opportunity to introduce Leopold to the family and, at the same time, find a way to bring up the Dorven situation. One evening, therefore, in the hotel lounge, the newly chosen brought gifts for the whole family. Inside a wreath of roses dedicated to his beautiful Adelina, he inserted a little card bearing a short message: *Love has come true one day. It is engraved in my heart where it will be forever.*

He and his lover went to be alone somewhere

- You have promised to marry me, haven't you Leo?

- Yes dear.

- What do you think if we announced our engagement?

- I have no objection, my love. I think that will help me a little bit.

- Thank you dear.

- Talk to me, do you have a plan in mind, a date set?

- No. I would not decide anything yet without your agreement first. Since you'll soon be leaving the country, we could enjoy celebrating our engagement here at the hotel.

- It's fantastic Adélina. You have dreams for both of us? Do you love me, dear?

- I have confessed it to you. You have an honored place reserved in my heart. But you know Leo, I've thought a lot about our situation.

- Thought?

- Yes Leo, I have to, she says, sighing.

- Adélina!

- Yes dear.

- Do you have at least an idea of what's going on inside me, how many times a day your name, only your name, makes my heart beat faster?

- I know my love, but you must admit that all men say the same words.

- Adélina, look at my eyes and you will realize my sincerity, because the eyes are windows to my mind.

She took his hand and put his palm on her heart.

- Your heart beats hard Adélina.

- In my heart I feel the breath of your mind. Take me with you, by your side Leo.

- Oh my love, I love you.

Tight in her lover's arms, she glanced tenderly at him.

- Adélina!

She raised her head and answered with longing eyes.

- Why can't I know the path that would lead me to your room?

- Well, you know; the one that leads to the door of my heart isn't it enough?

- Your lips are still closed, so far forbidden to me.

- My lips? Can they be tastier than yours?

- Do you want kiss my lips?

Then she closed her eyes, seized his mouth and kissed it.

- Take me; dear take me into your room, please.

- No dear. No. My room is forbidden to men.

- Take me, take me, please Adélina.

- No Leo, I tell you no. In my room there is a devil that might swallow you in one swoop.

- No Adélina! Take me, I don't care.

She got up, shook off her skirt.

- Follow me.

On the soft bed, they hugged. Their tongues came together in a warm kiss, as if from the heat of the night came from their lips. They felt transported, in a cloud as though they came from the breath of a strange body in another world. Their bodies, their souls became one.

- Let me have your soul in my body, I give you mine.

- Leopold! Leopold! You can't keep my soul.

- Why not, he says with closed eyes.

- Because it's poisoned.

They started caressing again, and became more excited. She lost control and was naked.

- Oh no Leo! No! No.

- Why Adélina? Why? You will be my wife. I swear before God who created us, I'll marry you. Nothing will stop me, nothing.

- I feel the strength of your love for me Leo. Your sincerity is reflected in the clarity of your conscience. Myself, I love you more than you could ever imagine, but…

- But what Adélina? What?

- Let's leave the bed, darling and sit on the sofa. She spoke with tears in her voice. She felt a fatal destiny. Seated near this man whose love was shining in his eyes, she was about to sink; then a torrent of tears coursed from her burning eyes, drowning her whole face.

-Are you crying dear? He said with a broken heart. His lips were trembling. I apologize from the bottom of my heart if I make you cry.

- You don't do anything wrong to me Leo, she said with tears in her throat.

- What will I become without you Adélina? Will I live? You are my complement on earth and even in eternity.

- My life is a long story Leo. All that matters is, do you love me?

- As you know my dear, I loved you since the first moment we exchanged glances. And even in the deepest darkness of death, I'll love you.

- May I speak? Are you listening?

- Who could listen to you better than I? Speak with me my love; tell me what you want, tell me anything, I'm listening.

- You aware that I was in love with somebody?

- Yes, I do my dear.

-Well, it happens that I am pregnant, and… and he and I broke off.

Leo became speechless, frozen. A vein in his left temple was throbbing. His eyes were filled with disappointment, and his face crumpled. Adélina continued to speak.

- Besides my pregnancy, there is worse.

- Worse? What else?

- My life is at risk. I am plagued with a virus that will take me away soon. Her cruel words, pronounced with hopelessness, struck Leo's heart like lead. His whole body was trembling.

- What is it Adélina? What are you talking about?

She remained curled on the sofa. Her makeup had faded away.

- What is the virus Adélina? Leo started again. Tell me, continue my dear, without fear. Whatever the virus, I'm with you. I am not like those followers of Jesus who turned their backs to him when he was before Pontius Pilate and on the way to Calvary. I am with you, I will always be with you; this is my promise, I swear, raising his hand.

- I am HIV positive. Don't say anything to anyone. Only my doctor and I know about it. It's for my benefit. If you really love me, you'll keep it secret.

Leo was quickly soaked with sweat. He was silent a long time. But he didn't have the courage to break his promise or give up that love. At the risk of his life, he will keep the promise he just made.

- You love me, I know Leo, but you are not obliged to commit yourself to such a dark road with someone who will soon disappear. I have enough courage to embrace my fate and go alone on the path of my destiny. I would never accept that you kill yourself because of me. I love you. I'm going to die, but you, you have to live. It won't be me, your murderer. You must stay alive Leo.

Leopold thought for a moment and exhaled a sigh, which came from the depths of his being.

- Can I see your doctor Adélina?

- My doctor? Yes, I think so.

- Call him tomorrow to make an appointment for both of us. Don't think I'll give up my promise, darling. Be sure I will be closer to you. I am on the road with you. Nothing is impossible on earth. We will live together. That's what I call the power of faith.

Three days later, the couple went to Dr. Pierrot to discuss the future of their union. Leopold wanted to take it to the end. The flame of love was about to consume him. They arrived on time. Miola was very nice to the couple. She received them warmly. The doctor was waiting for them eagerly. The enormous mahogany door creaked on its hinges. The doctor, standing by the window, waved to come in. The three entered the clinic lounge; then Adélina began.

- Dr. Pierrot this is Leopold, my future husband. Leopold, this is Dr. Pierrot, my longtime friend and my doctor.

The two men shook hands.

- Happy to meet you my dear friend, says the doctor.

- The pleasure is mine, thank you sir.

- I have been waiting anxiously. How are you Adélina, he says with a quick look.

- Up to today, excellent doctor. I feel quite well. Your advice has been effective. I don't know how to thank you.

- Don't worry my friend. It's my professional duty.

- Yes, as I told you doctor, we needed to see you today at the insistence of my fiancé.

- As long as I live I won't stop thanking you for saving Adelina. Your advice was perfect. Everyone sees me as an obsessed suitor; really I became lovesick since the first moment we exchanged glances; I had to go after her. As the Bible says, "Whoever seeks finds." Finally I am with her, and we're trying to work out a plan for the future. It's been three days since Adelina revealed her situation to me. I felt my head fall apart, and I was suddenly plunged into emptiness. As a doctor, her doctor, you're the only one who can tell us how long our life together will be.

The doctor grimaced, shook his head as if in pain. Adélina starts crying; hot tears were streaming down her face.

- Where are you living Leopold, inquired the doctor, here or abroad?

- I'm living in the U.S.

- Specifically, what are your plans with Adélina?

- I'll marry her.

Leaning his elbows on the desk with his head in his hands, Dr. Pierrot continued.

- You know Mr. Leopold, AIDS is a most terrible disease, the most terrifying. You're not a doctor, but you can understand the dilemma of a complicated disease that science can't defeat yet. A disease for which we have no vaccine or any drug. It's the most terrible danger that the world faces today. But life is life, unique. That is the reason we must fight to live. Twenty-three years old, this young lady is a sapling. Two things can help her out. First, her morale is very strong, second, her blood type, O positive. In the U.S. currently there are effective drugs that can treat the virus, restore the immune system. Someone with this blood type, like your fiancée, can resist the virus for more than forty years, depending on the treatment. So there is hope Mr. Leopold.

The lover turned his eyes to his fiancée with a smile filled with joy and hope. And through the mirror of his sight, life was shining like the sun at the horizon.

- But, very important, the doctor added, you always have to use condoms for your protection. Even in your dreams, don't dare forget. Another thing, so far, only you and I know she is HIV positive. Let's keep it secret until she wants....

Leopold moved toward Dr. Pierrot, hugged him and patted him on the back. Adélina came closer and embraced him.

- Tell me I am not dreaming Dr. Pierrot. You are a source of hope, and whenever I've come to you, I am always relieved. God will protect you and your family. The almighty God will watch our life. On my faith, we'll serve Him one day.

Releasing the doctor, Adélina went to her lover. They hugged each other, shared some warm kisses. The doctor admired them, smiling.

- You are the image of love. What a beautiful couple!

- Thank you doctor, they answered in chorus.

The sun blazed its torrid rays over the city. The white car drove slowly. Some passersby were moving along the sidewalks.

- Adélina.

- Oh! Yes dear, as she was jolted by a bump.

- You are so pensive my love. What are you thinking about— our marriage?

- Eh... my marriage? Last time we were speaking of an engagement.

- I think otherwise today.

- Really!

- I think of marrying you immediately, any objection to that?

- Not at all, my love. Why did you change your mind so quickly?

- You... I hope you can understand. He thought for a moment. I will not return to the U.S. without marrying you. Time is money, we can't waste it....

- As you please Leo.

- Let's tell your parents about it.

- Why darling?

- Because we must plan the wedding.

CHAPTER XVII

Golden rays burst from the saffron sun. With streets under noisy construction, there was dust in the air and it was suffocating. On the balconies with wrought iron, some men with bleak faces sat with the daily paper opened wide in their hands. This has been the most popular one in the city for a century. On the front page, a big script of black crow:

The man in the deadly sting, the grisly genocide of all time

This is the worst disaster Haiti has experienced, reported the paper, since the arrival of the AIDS pandemic in the early 1980s. This is the veil of a horrible night of darkness that inhales death around the city on the east side, through a libido carrying its poisoned sting. It's too terrible and fatal, frankly. A man named Dorven Marc Forest, forty-two years old, a brand new millionaire obviously, returned to his country, luggage filled, bank account full of money, but with blood infected with a fatal virus.

Mr. Marc Forest young, very handsome, lives in a wonderful house like a mansion on the heights of Furcy. His entire childhood was spent in Bel-Air, a slum whose dark and miserable appearance is exposed to the world as the image of poverty.

He is the son of a working man still living in a sordid shack. He broke relations with his family the first day he entered the United States of America. Becoming miraculously rich, he returned home with the sadistic idea of infecting girls by exploiting their poverty; poor girls facing terrible hardships in life. And so goes the slogan: Life in exchange for a handful of dollars.

Rumors report that the virus carrier has already infected hundreds of girls that he welcomed to his mansion at Furcy.

With regard to this criminal act of Mr. Dorven Marc Forest, the picture is very gloomy.

The patient, in serious condition, was discharged to his relatives by the hospital.

The TV was on and the screen mottled with light. A large T with the tail of and I formed the logo TI covering the screen. Suddenly, a purple light flashed, dropping each letter forming TELE IMAGE. At the center, a slogan appeared: TELEIMAGE to Entertain You. The series started with three commercials. Then the host of "Coup de Foudre" began his daily program.

- Ladies and gentlemen good evening. I am Pierre Médard. Today is Thursday the 30th... As you know each Thursday at this time, I am the host of the very exciting show, the very popular "Coup de Foudre". Our topic this evening will be a hot discussion, but rich in information I hope: AIDS and its origin. We remind you that this discussion follows the sad misfortune that has hit Haitian youth: the Dorven case. Ladies and gentlemen we have some very important guests tonight, such as the Rev. Pastor Marc Dalmond. The religious man was wearing a light blue suit and a red shirt, white collar around his neck and his Bible in hand. Continued to list his guesses, the host Medard added: Dr Frantz Vieux. With us also are Dr Frébat Mbarré, a Gambian-born scientist; Dr. Philippe Desrang, the minister of public health and Dr. Bernard Guinaudeau, a Canadian researcher. Ladies and gentlemen, continued the host, dear viewers, remember that at the end of the twentieth century, beginning in the 1980s to be more precise, a terrible virus hit our world and inflicted a lot of damage. Since the beginning of the world, no disease, no pandemic had been as cruel and fatal as AIDS. AIDS, an immunodeficiency syndrome makes the human body weak and vulnerable to infections. On every continent, casualties are enormous. Ironically, the Haitian people have been stigmatized, targeted by the U.S., France and Canada among others. Haitians have been called a "group at risk" for the AIDS pandemic. While this injustice prevails, everyone in our society has his opinion. For some, this evil does not even exist. They say it's only a manipulation of society. Others see the virus as punishment by a wrathful God. Pastor Marc Dalmond, a theologian, professor and man of God will tell us more about that thesis. Good evening Pastor.

The Pastor cleared his throat.

- Pardon, thank you Pierre; viewers, good evening.

- Pastor Dalmond, we begin our program with you tonight. How do you see the ravages of this virus in our society?

- Well, it must be admitted that opinions are very mixed on the actual state of this virus in Haiti and throughout the world. The Bible is the first and only guide for anyone who devotes himself to serve God. Iniquitous people don't remain unpunished, the Bible says. The sinner will pay for his transgression until his fourth generation. A close look at the past leads us to Egyptian antiquity to see the growing wounds on Pharaoh's Egypt due to injustice inflicted on the people of God and disobedience to His prophet. We can easily understand the destruction of the cities Sodom and Gomorrah because of corruption throughout the whole nation. Finally came a period of grace in the year thirty-three of our era. The Messiah predicted this miserable and difficult time of terror, crime, famine and war across the world. Nothing surprises us, we Christians. Evil is following its course like always. It is the wrath of God hanging over us.

- Thank you Pastor.

The camera focused on the entire panel.

- You're watching, ladies and gentlemen, TV Image. We remind you that our topic tonight is a discussion on AIDS. Now we turn to the Minister of Public Health, Dr. Philippe Desrang. Good evening doctor, welcome to our program "Coup de Foudre" on TV Image.

- Thank you Pierre, good evening to you all.

- Dr. Desrang, as the minister of public health for our country, what is your plan vis-à-vis the disease, which has begun to decimate our youth?

- First Mr. Médard, before saying anything, let me congratulate you for addressing this issue of far-reaching concern, moderated with sensitive concern. A job well done. It is for the benefit of our people, and a source of pride for the government.

- Thank you! He says in his countertenor voice.

- I am deeply concerned, said the health minister in a calm tone, that our youth are facing this global challenge and are prey to this fatal and incurable disease. And, as a health official of this country, I have the duty to intervene for a minimum of care for young people at the mercy of this disease. We must be honest and say that previous governments have left a sad legacy: no health-care program— the files are empty; nothing we could follow whatsoever. We cannot just complain. We have to do something. Our government is young. Our health team is working late at night to control the virus that has spread all over the country.

- What do you say about the allegations of the media in Western countries, especially England, France, the U.S., Canada in collaboration with organizations such as the Canadian Red Cross and U.S. research centers accusing us of carrying the virus?

- You know Mr. Médard, since the birth of our nation; we as a people have been always under fire from these powerful nations. This is unfortunate, frankly. Perhaps, we are doomed to be manipulated by foreign countries. What can we do?

- Good evening Doctor Vieux, do you have something to add to the minister's remarks?

-Thank you Pierre, good evening to all Haitian viewers. Let's say that AIDS came as a weapon with both biological and psychological aspects. I was in Paris the 17th of June 1983, busy dining with a French friend, a doctor too. She gave me the daily paper *Le Monde* that she had been reading. Turning to the medicine section, which is my domain, a headline caught my attention: "The Prevention of AIDS in France." I read as follows: "AIDS, acquired immunodeficiency syndrome will reach more homosexual and bisexual men with multiple partners, intravenous drug users, people originating from Haiti and equatorial Africa as well as sexual partners (men or women) of persons belonging to these categories." The article was signed J. Ives Nau.

- What was your reaction, doctor?

- I did not know how to respond, frankly. I said she probably read the article and wanted me to read it too. I concluded that if the mad men— white people of the West— declare a racial war against us, we have no recourse.

- Now, Pierre says as he turns to another panelist, let's put the discussion in a research context. This is Dr. Frébat Mbarré, scientist and researcher, working in the field of infectious disease at the Sorbonne University.

Dr. Mbarré, "Coup de Foudre" and the whole team of TV Image thank you for coming. We know that you are the head of a very competent and zealous team of researchers. I think this evil called AIDS that's ravaging the world could be at the center of your concerns.

- Thank you Pierre, and good evening to you all. Let me begin by saying that scientific research must be accurate, never based on absurd statements. Science also accepts its limitations. No research center is up to the challenge of this evil afflicting youth throughout the world. Early in 1983, I saw in newspapers that people in countries like Haiti and in equatorial Africa, also individuals in same-sex relationships, are considered groups at risk for carrying the virus. It is also unfortunate that there is still a great deal of speculation. According to the information from the Center for Disease Control (CDC) in Atlanta, the rate of infection date is the following: homosexuals 72%, intravenous drug users 17%, Haitian immigrants 4%, hemophiliacs 1%, and non-categorized individuals 6%. I think it is unprofessional for researchers to approach a scientific matter lightly and maliciously. I don't have the right to mislead anyone. I think that such accusations are nothing but intrigue to hide the origin of the disease on the one hand, and political and ideological manipulation on the other.

- Thank you Dr. Mbarré, you know, this is a discussion in which we try to involve as many people as possible. I'll return to you later. Now let's introduce Dr. Guinaudau. Good evening doctor.

- Thank you Pierre and good evening to the viewers.

- Dr. Guinaudeau, you are a medical researcher working for one of the largest research centers in Canada. Can you tell us about any difficulties as a black scientist you encountered in this journey?

- You ask me a thorny question Pierre. To be honest with you, if I had to tell you about difficulties from my medical studies through to this research center, it would take years. Maybe I could write a ton of books. The most important thing is that by saving lives, I give meaning to my life. So I think I've chosen a sacred career.

- Could you tell us a little bit about the direction of your work in this research center?

- I have committed myself to the research center for fifteen years, particularly in infectious diseases. The past five years my work has been focused on the mystery of the AIDS pandemic.

- You talk about the mystery of the AIDS pandemic; it's a big word for me.

- Ah yes, a big word in the sense of the dynamic manipulation, plot and fuss around this disease. With racism, political agendas and ostracism, our race becomes the target of an ideological war. We are the first victims. And we have no other alternative than to fight, whatever the price may be.

- Ladies and gentlemen, dear viewers who follow TV Image. We remind you that our discussion this evening is AIDS and its origin. We have a relatively large panel: a pastor, the minister of public health, a Haitian physician and three medical researchers.

- Mr. Mbarré, has research led to information of interest?

- I believe that we must begin at the beginning, with history. In 1925 US government did not ratify the Geneva Convention prohibiting chemical and biological warfare. Between 1941 and 1955, the birth rate went up enormously. The return of soldiers from World War Two triggered the baby boom. Between 1957 and 1990, population doubled. It was obvious that individual behavior had to be controlled to guarantee human survival. That was the reason the superpowers agreed to focus on this problem. By 1957, research in Huntsville, Alabama confirmed data that an explosion of birth rate was possible. They also suggested that pollution of the high atmosphere and the hole in the ozone layer could cause an unprecedented catastrophe and reduced human survival after 2000. Because they wanted to avoid a population explosion, the devils of this world advocated a massive population reduction. That was the reason US leaders formulated a global disarmament plan. The U.S. Disarmament Agency (UDA) was founded. In 1957, President Dwight Eisenhower said this: "Infant mortality is reduced; life expectancy increased, and hunger in the world decreased. Those facts announce an eventual explosion of world population, which will double within a generation."

This leads to three alternatives. Alternative one: Explode a nuclear bomb in the stratosphere where excessive heat would carbonize the planet. Alternative two: Build subterranean cities. Alternative three: Inhabit other planets, Mars for example.

In 1968, the Cooperative Organization Report (COR) calculated how to achieve population reduction: decrease the birth rate and increase the death rate. In order to decrease the birth rate, medical measures such as contraception and abortion were increased. From 1965 to 1980, the cost of this project ran from US $2.1 to 185 million. Between 1981 and

1989, the Agency for International Development (AID) spent more than three billion dollars for the same project. Seventy-five percent of the contraceptives were distributed in third-world countries. Groups such as women's and homosexuals' liberation movements received significant funds. To reduce the Brazilian population to 30 million by 2000, between 20 and 25 million young women were sterilized against their will. That was a major scandal in 1992. In some districts in Brazil, 60% of women were sterilized. The Brazilian Minister of Public Health, Dr. Guerra, was shocked and angrily condemned this. "This sterilization program is the cruelest one in the world, as far as birth control is concerned." He denounced several organizations that supported this program, such as the Ford Foundation, Rockefeller Foundation, Population Council and AID.

Other attempts to eliminate population could include use of tobacco. In the US, many tobacco products exported throughout the world were grown in fields contaminated with radioactive uranium. This further endangered smokers throughout the world. An important increase of trachea, lung, mouth and lip cancer was observed. Malathion, for instance, an insecticide for crops and fruit, was spread over populations by Central of Intelligential Autonomous (CIA) helicopters. CIA headquarters in Evergreen, Arizona had been receiving drugs from Central America. A death-rate alternative was also taken seriously. This is why the ruling American elite considered nuclear war, but the most practical solution would be an epidemic, with Mother Nature solely responsible.

The Club of Rome, under the direction of Aurelio Pecceyi, was already working on such project and proposing others. The objective was to develop a virus that would destroy the immune system. No vaccine would be able to help. They wanted to inject it in the mass population and protect the elite. Once the population is decimated, they will officially develop treatment for the survivors. This project, part of the Global 2000 Plan, was indeed the beginning of AIDS made from the manipulation of human micro-organisms. This project called MK-NAOMI, passed in the American Congress in 1969 under the resolution HB-15090, with US $10 million to launch it. The US Ministry of Defense sent it to Fort Detrick to be implemented.

- But who is in charge of protecting the population if not the government?

- And the most shocking part is that by the end of World War Two in 1945, many pathogens effective against human beings, animals and plants had been studied and experimental tests performed. In 1947 they created the OSD, Office Section of Defense to supervise technical research. An ad hoc committee on chemical and biological warfare had been formed to control the OSD. In 1948, the committee reported on special operations in biological warfare, concluding that the use of biological weapons for subversive purposes was entirely possible. And the recommendations of the committee were accepted, which began the secret experiments of the US Army.

- A statement really full of information. But as a matter of fact, inquired the host, what was all this for?

- You will be surprised to know that in 1949, the largest experimental with a capacity of one million liters of pathogen agents was built at the Detrick Camp. The same year they started testing projectiles and explosive pathogenic organisms. In 1950, in Arkansas, the US Army began to build a biological unit agent in Pine Bluff. The plant became operational in spring 1954. The total cost was $90 million, and the plant was capable of producing various pathogens including brucellosis and tularemia, a disease of rabbits transmissible to humans. In1962, the project 112 Work Group, established in 1961, gave a detailed report of draft tests of biological and chemical weapons. The same project operated at Fort Douglas, the Central Test of the Desert (DTC). The center was to maintain continual liaison with the Department of Public Health of the US to evaluate experiments with biological and chemical weapons. In 1967, the Pine Bluff laboratories released several types of infectious microorganisms. In 1978, following an agreement between Fort Detrick and the New YK Blood Center (NYBC) in Manhattan, more than one thousand homosexuals were recruited by government scientists to serve as subjects for trials of a hepatitis B vaccine. The vaccinations were administered at the NYBC. In 1979 the first AIDS case was detected in a homosexual vaccinated at NYBC. Toward 1984, 70% of the thousand homosexuals vaccinated tested HIV positive.

- Dr. Vieux, they have stigmatized us, we Haitians as a group at risk, carrying the virus; where is the truth in all this?

- The truth Mr. Médard isn't as veiled as we think. We just need to use documents and scientific materials to find it. It was a plan to exterminate blacks and some other groups in modern society, including Hispanics and homosexuals. Dr. William Campbell Douglas, in his book *AIDS: The End of Civilization* states, "The world was startled when the *London Times* reported on its front page May 11, 1987 that the World Help Organization (WHO) had 'triggered' the AIDS epidemic in Africa through the WHO smallpox immunization program. The only people in the free world not surprised by the *London Times* front page exposé were the Americans, because they never heard about it...."

According to the *London Times* article, "Smallpox Vaccine Triggered AIDS Virus," by Pearce Wright: "The greatest spread of HIV infection coincides with the most intense immunization program, with the number of people immunized as follows: Zaire 36,878,000; Zambia 19,060,000; Tanzania 14,972,000; Uganda 11,616,000; Malawi 8,118,000; Rwanda 3,382,000 and Burundi 3,274,000. Pearce Wright also notes that Brazil was included in the eradication campaign and that about 14,000 Haitians working for the UN in Central Africa were also infected. Mr. Pearce also writes, "Charity and health workers are convinced that millions of new AIDS cases are about to hit southern Africa."

After a meeting of 50 experts near Geneva this month, it was revealed that up to 75 million people, one third of the population could contract the disease within the next five years. And we know that due to inhumane South African white supremacy, the Africans will be isolated. This will intensify an AIDS outbreak by confining the infected into small crowded towns where it will be almost impossible to contain its spread. There have been over 50 thousand deaths in Africa already, and it is conservatively believed that close to 75million African people could be infected. You're asking me about the truth, I am not responding by lying. The truth is, as planned by the world's superpowers to reduce global population by limiting births and increasing deaths, some populations were targeted, particularly we black people. And, the question one must ask is why is the victim accused while the real criminal is protected and not held accountable for his terrible and infamous crimes?

- Ah yes! A crazy planet given to the criminals, and also your exposé is telling the truth of the history, said host Medard.

- Thus, Mr. Tod Wiss, at a seminar on AIDS in Lennox Hospital in 1983 I attended said: "As daring as it may seem, given the attitudes toward homosexuals and others, the possible use of biological weapons must be seriously considered." Shortly before, Senator Wiss, Robert Harris and Jeremy Paxman in their book, *A Higher Form of Killing*, published in 1982, wrote: "Since 1962, 40 scientists employed in biological warfare laboratories of the NAA enjoyed their fulltime scientific research." The implications became clear seven years later when a spokesman for the Department of Public Health of the US said that genetic manipulation could solve the problem with biological warfare; that is to say, the limited variety of diseases. With strong evidence, we can conclude that AIDS is a disease made in the laboratories of the West by the lords of hell.

- A serious atrocity, isn't it doctor?

- Ah yes, and the famous Coué method is the sharpest psychological weapon used by the mad men of the West when they want to perpetrate their lies through slander: Repeat it incessantly and it will eventually become truth. But in fact, even ten thousand times told, a lie is a lie, nothing else. And the objective of this malice was to decimate blacks in the human race, because having been victims of systematic servitude for centuries; we are ready to be eradicated from the earth, which they think they own.

- Dr. Guinaudeau, do you know similar research, asked Médard.

- Dr. William C. Douglass writing in the December 1987 edition of *Heal Consciousness* entitled "WHO Murdered Africa" is emphatic that the World Health Organization used Africa as the test ground for the deadly man-made virus. The major question is why would anyone want to do this. I think that the answer is rather simple when reading this release from Moscow, published in the *Herald Examiner*, June 6, 1987: "Soviets charge US has germ weapon to kill blacks. Moscow-US Information Agency Director Charles Wick said he broke off talks yesterday with the chief of a Soviet news agency over claims that the Central Intelligence Agency (CIA) has a biological weapon for killing blacks. Wick said at a news conference at US headquarters that he received a cable from Washington on Thursday about a dispatch from the

Novosti News agency that asserted the Central Intelligence Agency had developed an ethnic weapon. Summarizing the story, Wick said it claimed that the CIA agents employ gas in developing countries and that the latest is an ethnic weapon of pathogens which are lethal for the Africans…." Right after the vote of the MK-NAOMI project by the American Congress in 1969, scientists and the government said before the AS commission, "A synthetic biologic agent should be developed, which doesn't exist naturally. It should be able to destroy the human immune system. It's possible to develop this within 5 to 10 years. It must be resistant to any immunologic therapy." According to the detailed explanations of Dr. Theodore A Strecker, the AIDS virus made at Fort Detrick was mixed with a fatal bovine leukemia and the visna virus of sheep. The famous Dr. Strecker had the courage to denounce that criminal project. But still they started targeting homosexuals, blacks and Hispanics. The World Health Organization (WHO) and the National Cancer Institute (NCI) were regular contributors to this inhumane project.

In 1972, WHO explained its position: "We do research because we need to know if some viruses can destroy immune system functions." In short, let's make a virus that can destroy autoimmune T cells. Through the vaccination campaign against smallpox by WHO in 1997, a large portion of Africa became infected with AIDS. Dr. Strecker made it clear: "Without some tough medicines, the whole African continent will be devastated in 15 years." Under Dr. Wolf Mugner, director of the Centers for Disease Control (CDC), and the vaccination program for hepatitis B, segments of the American population were contaminated with the AIDS virus. The homosexuals were the first. The AIDS vaccine with leukemia visna virus was made in Phoenix, Arizona. The Swiss company Bilder Berger directed this criminal program, which included the H. Kissinger Depopulation Policy (HKDP). According to this, third-world countries had to reduce and control their populations in order to continue receiving funds from the U. S. Any noncompliant country would face war, according to the CIA.

- Do you agree, doctor, that at Fort Detrick in Maryland, the NAA is developing a major chemical and biological arsenal?

- It's clear that Fort Detrick has the largest arsenal of biological weapons in the world, with an area of 1,400 hectares of land and a staff of 900 scientists and more than 1,000 civilian employees. Eighty-five percent of what is produced is classified, and fifteen percent is released to placate the general public. Humankind faces the most dangerous era inexistence. Chemical and biological weapons are terrible threats to our world. Robin Clark in his book *The Silent Weapons* alleged: "The men of science, working in research on biological warfare… made microorganisms more stable, more virulent, more infectious and less susceptible to drugs and antibiotics. Their work had been rightly qualified as public health countdown."

- We're going to close our discussion, but not without your last thoughts Dr. Mbarré, because your revelations are so well documented, very well done.

- Well! And I think we have learned about the AIDS virus, and Haitians as victims have learned a lot tonight. The Commission on Population Policy was founded in 1975 by U.S. Secretary of State Henry Kissinger. From the same group came the Globe 2000 Report given by hand to American President Jimmy Carter. Thomas Fergus, head of the US Office of Public Affairs for Latin America stated: "Only one thing matters for us, we must reduce population density. Either they do it our way, that's to say with proper methods, (AIDS, sterilization) or they undergo massacres like in Salvador or Beirut. Over population is a political problem. If we can't control it, we will be in deep trouble. We must be authoritarian, even fascist if need be, in order to solve this crucial problem. Professionals refuse to help us because of humanitarian reasons. That's all right, but it's a matter of raw materials and environmental factors. For strategic purposes, we must follow this path. Salvador is one example among many that shows our failure in population reduction, which leads to a severe national crisis. The Salvadorian government did not succeed in reducing its population using our methods, which is the reason civil war took place. There was population relocation and some food rationing. However, the problem still remains. The civil war was the last attempt. Now the fastest way to reach our goal is to create a famine in Africa, or an epidemic such as the Black Death, which definitely will wipe out the Salvadorians." Fergus continued, "We target a country and impose a plan of development. Throw it away and take care of your population reduction. If you disagree with the planning process, you will be another Salvador or a second Cambodia. Something had to occur in Salvador, the birth rate is 3.3%, the highest in the world. In 21 years, the population of the Salvador will double. The civil war can help us stop it if it's done on a large scale."

In April 1968 studies from COR, started in 1957 at the request of Aurelio Pecceyi, and were released. *The Population Bomb*, published in 1968, proposed some solutions. "To summarize, we must say that the world population is still growing, because the birth rate is higher than the death rate. It's very simple. There are two solutions. Either we reduce the birth rate or increase the death rate. It was imperative from the beginning to strictly control births, to avoid the second solution."

To conclude, Aurelio Pecceyi affirmed that if he became infected from the microbes, he wouldn't seek treatment. He would be a hero. Programming this criminal project, MK-NAOMI or AIDS, was by the Massachusetts Institute of Technology (MIT). Speaking of the project, B. Russell mentioned: "You say the difficult periods are somehow particular, which means we have to take particular approaches. In the beginning of the industrial revolution, it was feasible, but now, it's not, unless we reduce the population growth significantly.... The traditional war is not the proper way to do it. The bacterial war would be more practical and effective. If every generation was experiencing the plague, the survivors could grow up without endangering the global equilibrium." Dr. J. Coleman explained in autumn 1994 in Honolulu: "The new virus, more powerful and violent than AIDS, has been tested during one year in a South American country. It can be spread all over in spring 1995. Once active, it will infect you in the morning and kill you in the afternoon. In an article from the Swiss magazine *Zeit & Schrift* in December 1994 about over population was the following statement:" There are signs that aliens, technologically advanced, have given the key to the human genetic code to some scientists. At least 30 fatal viruses have existed for30 years or more. There is no treatment for these viruses, except an electromagnetic approach, Scalar Technology. The US has been aware of it since 1947. Scientists have access to it in case of infection.

- Do you have a final word, Dr Vieux?
- Going back to the age of the so-called discovery of the Americas, toward the end of the 15th century, the genocide perpetrated against Native Americans by the Europeans could be considered the worst extermination in history. They decimated 75million Amerindians. Thus, one might deduce that man's hatred for his brothers inspires the worst evil in his heart. But God always protects the innocent. This is how His will has been expressed since creation. As witnesses today, victims of the sadism of madmen, we are not going to bow down obediently, as a passive people, to accept those shameful lies. They have spread their slander about us across the world as the source of this viral disease; we will throw it back to them. Aware that they control all mass media, the international press, we know the battle will be difficult, but we won't give up.

CHAPTER XVIII

The wet sky became cloudier, and the contours of the mountains were sometimes gray, sometimes darkgreen, on the horizon. The dark sky threatened thunderous rain. Mother Nature soon will drop her anger on every living thing. All the radio stations are broadcasting news about the hurricane that will hit Haiti in a few hours. Florida has suffered severe damage: 13 dead, 50 missing, 10,000 homeless, about 17,000 cars swept away and neighborhoods without electricity. Panama had a powerful blow with 37 deaths, more than 400 missing, 5,000 homeless.... The wind was gusting in Havana at 120 mph. The Cuban government declared a state of emergency last night. Haiti's buildings are not strong enough to resist the hurricane, although its velocity has diminished. One station said that it started to weaken after the Dominican coast. Suddenly a white glimmer appeared from the west. The sun pierced the sky like a candle flame in a mass of darkness. The wind continued to stir the trees that already lost branches, broken on the ground with scattered leaves. Violent dusty air mixed with debris, a jumble of twigs and dead leaves, swept into the streets and blurred the outlines of the houses.

Adélina raised the curtain of the east window. She gently half-opened the adjacent door, took a look outside. The sky was completely clouded and the air polluted.

- It's terrible, frankly, she says breathing deeply.

- What's so terrible Adélina? Asked her sister, who abruptly came into the living room.

- Oh! Didn't you look outside?

- A very bad day for you, to tell the truth, I don't understand. They remain quiet a moment. You're so pretty my sister, she adds with emotional tenderness. In this world there are people who are born different from others.

- Not really, she replies, smiling, but with a forced smile.

The dress wasn't specifically made for a wedding. A fringed gown tailored for her with notches in the neck and sleeves highlights her svelte body. With her ebony hair gathered into a chignon, she was so elegant. Her shiny black shoes with medium heels enhanced her height. She wore simple make-up.

The weather swept by sunshine found its bright spot, but one eye was half-open and shy. The wind reduced its fury.

Despite the threat of the weather, the whole household was ready.

The black limousine parked next to the house. Leopold came out; Adélina joined him. A team of photographers hurried to get out of a car and began shooting the couple everywhere in different poses. The parents of both families accompanied them in the long black car, which took off....

- My children, the pastor continued to shout; here you are in the house of God to marry. I wish you happiness in abundance. You will be blessed, I am sure. But be aware that life has two poles that you must be ready to deal with. You are united for better and for worse. Before families and friends, and on behalf of the authority that God has granted to me, I declare you husband and wife. Then he placed the rings on their fingers, and commanded them to kiss each other.

After his four-months sojourn for the sole purpose of winning Adélina, finally Leopold returned to the U.S. He went only for one week, just to supervise his company! His marriage made him joyful, blissful, and happy for the first time in his life. It's obviously crazy to marry a sick girl. It is stubborn and risky at the same time. The true meaning of life can only be found in the beloved one who pleases your heart. Joy softens the heart and strengthens the soul with hope. Really, there is nothing like love. Being with the one you love is fabulous ecstasy, a dream world...a world of happiness.

She accompanied her husband to the airport. They were both pensive, plunging them into sadness.
- As long as I live far from you I will be lifeless.

- You are all my strength Leo, the giant on whom I place my entire burden. Your absence will be painful. I already feel the emptiness in me. I need your support, you know.

- Our telephone conversations won't be enough, I admit, but I will do my best to be with you in spirit; this way, you'll be strong and calm.

- This will be my first night not sleeping on your chest. I have a crush on you. I'm spoiled. You are my husband forever; I'll die in your arms.

- We will be together again. You won't die, my darling. Death is a dark word that should be out of your mind.

- Will I grow old with you Leo?

- Why not? Stop thinking of death.

- Despite all the doctor's advice, sometimes I feel weak and depressed.

- I don't doubt it, my love, because you are human.

At the airport they were still hugging each other, kissing for a few moments. They couldn't hold their tears, trying to dry them while gazing each other. The airplane took off like a bird, carrying Leopold in the air, while the white car brought Adélina back home.

Two years later, what everybody expected from the man whose return to the country caused so much damage, happened. For sometime now, the Marc Forest family had moved to the prodigal son's house in Furcy. They became so caring of Dorven, and gave him all possible support, because they didn't have room in their heart for bitterness, hatred, especially for blood relatives.

The house reflected the sinister image of death. The face of everyone was filled with sorrow. Dorven will soon be gone. He has endured much during these two years. His body was dried flesh, immobile and skeletal. His glassy eyes, lost in their orbits, do not flash anymore. On the large bed in the oval room, he barely could move. The echo of his cough made his chest vibrate. It was very dry. He waved his mother to come to him. They both began crying and torrents of hot tears flooded their faces.

- My son, my son, caressing his face with her fingers.

- I'll soon leave Mom; I'm not in this world anymore. Where is my father?

- He is not too far from us; I'll call him.

His vision had almost gone; he could not even see his father bedside the large bed.

- Dad… Dad, I… I hope you forgive my sins and… and that you forgive me so that I can leave in peace.

- I forgive you my son.

- You… you are in charge of my funeral. Be modest. A… avoid spending too… only a simple funeral.

He pulled out an envelope from under his pillow, and handed it to him.

- Everything is in there; the deed and the bank accounts. Where is Sabine?

- I'm here, near you big brother. He took the girl's hand, put it in his, staring at her, then his head fell to the left.

It was the day of Adélina's departure. Accompanied by her beautiful daughter Adeline, fifteen months old, she was to join her beloved Leopold in New York. The suitcases were ready. The whole family, in the living room, was present. The radio began playing a funereal melody: "We announce with infinite sorrow the sad news of the passing of Mr. Dorven Marc Forest at the age of 44, in his residence at Furcy. In these painful circumstances, our sympathy and sincere condolences to his mother, Mrs. Germain Marc Forest, born Julie Lundy; his father, Mr. Germain Marc Forest; to his young sister, Miss Sabine Marc Forest; his two brothers, Guy and Georges Marc Forest; and his former fiancée, Ms Adélina Beaujour.... God rest his soul."